The Sorrowful Eyes
of Hannah Karajich

The Sorrowful Eyes
of Hannah Karajich

Ivan Olbracht

Translated by Iris Urwin Lewitová

Introduction by Miroslav Holub

CENTRAL EUROPEAN UNIVERSITY PRESS

Budapest London New York

First published in Czechoslovakia as part of *Golet v údoli*
First published in English in 1967 by Crown Publishers, Inc.,
in a collection of stories entitled
The Bitter and the Sweet

This edition first published in 1999 by
Central European University Press

An imprint of the
Central European University Share Company
Nádor utca 11, H-1051 Budapest, Hungary
Tel: +36-1-327-3138 or 327-3000
Fax: +36-1-327-3183
E-mail: ceupress@ceu.hu
Website: www.ceupress.com

400 West 59th Street, New York NY 10019, USA
Tel: +1-212-547-6932
Fax: +1-212-548-4607
E-mail: mgreenwald@sorosny.org

This edition and notes © Central European Classics Trust, 1999
Introduction © Miroslav Holub, 1998

ISBN 963 9116 47 5
ISSN 1418-0162

Library of Congress Cataloging in Publication Data
A CIP catalog record for this book is available upon request

Printed in Hungary by
Akadémiai Nyomda, Martonvásár

The Sorrowful Eyes
of Hannah Karajich

The Sorrowful Eyes
of Hannah Karajich

Ivan Olbracht

Translated by Iris Urwin Lewitová

Introduction by Miroslav Holub

CENTRAL EUROPEAN UNIVERSITY PRESS

Budapest   London   New York

This edition first published in 1999 by Central European University Press
H-1051, Október 6. utca 12.

First published in Czechoslovakia as part of *Golet v údoli*
First published in English in the United States of America in 1967
by Crown Publishers, Inc. in a collection of stories entitled
The Bitter and the Sweet

Distributed by
Central European University Press Marketing Department
H-1051 Budapest, Október 6. utca 12. Hungary
Tel: 36-1-327-3138 or 327-3014, Fax: 36-1-327-3183
E-mail: ceupress@osi.hu

In UK, Ireland and Western Europe, Plymbridge Distributors Ltd,
Estover Road, Plymouth, PL6 7PZ, United Kingdom
Tel: 44-1752-202301, Fax: 44-1752-202333
E-mail: orders@plymbridge.com

ISBN 963 9116 47 5
ISSN 1418-0162

Library of Congress Cataloguing in Publication Data
A CIP catalog record for this book is available from the
Library of Congress

Printed and bound in Hungary
by Akadémiai Nyomda Kft.

Contents

Introduction

There is an old story about a Hasidic Jew being asked how many countries he has seen. Well, he says, I was born in Austria-Hungary, I was married in Czechoslovakia, I was widowed in Hungary, and now I'm trying to make ends meet in the Soviet Union. Been quite a traveller then, haven't you? Not at all. I never moved a step from Mukachevo.

Mukachevo is in Sub-Carpathian Ruthenia, a region that belonged to Austria-Hungary until 1918, to Czechoslovakia between the wars, to Hungary again during the Second World War, to the Soviet Union after 1945, and is now part of the Ukraine. That remote, troubled region is the setting for this extraordinary book. In Czechoslovak nostalgia, Sub-Carpathian Ruthenia is something like a pearl resting at the bottom of the ocean, something barely found before again being lost, a sixth finger amputated before we had learnt to use it. And we are still feeling the phantom pain. By our standards it is a wild country, 'beautiful in its poverty' as a poet put it, a land that could have been closer to us than to any of its rulers.

Hasidic Jews had been immigrating there from Galicia ever since the eighteenth century, along with their language and orthodox religious rituals, less strict than the Talmudistic ones and emphasising personal mystic experiences, but none the less mandatory and immutable, if only because that was a way of survival and the only hope of the weak and abandoned. The mountain villages were isolated and inward-looking. Migration, or indeed communication between them was extremely rare. Of the Jews in Sub-Carpathia, 20 per cent lived in total poverty without any property whatsoever. Sixty-five per cent of them owned small shops, taverns, workshops and their own small houses. The rest were 'capitalists' who had escaped from the standard Ruthenian occupations of cattle-grazing and woodcutting, and attached themselves to the rulers of the moment. They lived among Ruthenians, Hungarians, Czechs, Slovaks and a few Germans and Romanians.

Only one in three of the Jews survived the Holocaust. At the end of the war, the Hungarian fascist regime preferred to sacrifice the poor Sub-Carpathian Jews rather than the wealthy Jews of Budapest. Their deportation began under the personal supervision of Adolf Eichmann within three weeks of the German invasion of Hungary, on 7 April 1944. After that there was nothing left to make the eyes of Jewish girls sad.

In July 1945, I and a group of student friends set out to discover this amputated land. On foot, we reached the Ruthenian village of Ruský Potok. In a deep valley between forests and mountain pastures, on steep hillsides, there was a cluster of wooden shacks with

thatched roofs and tiny windows. They were picturesque and poor – the two, as is well known, being in-
separable. In a few of the windows there was still glass;
in others we glimpsed the terrified faces of women and
children to whom anything strange was a portent of
further disaster. In the mud on the village green a few
geese were waddling about, so dirty that they looked
like grouse, along with a creature halfway between a pig
and a dog. We sneaked into one of the shacks and found
a floor of trampled clay, a table, an invalid chair, a few
logs, one bed for the grown-ups and a large crate of hay
serving as the children's bedroom. There was a sour
smell of wet fur, ingrained smoke and emptiness.

From the tavern on the edge of Ruský Potok came the
sound of muted uproar. Inside, a Jew with a black hat
and what had once been a jacket was the barman – a
strange survivor of the Holocaust. He was pouring out
a sticky liquid, in which some flies seemed to be wading,
for Ruthenian woodcutters who were already at the
glassy-eyed and gibbering stage. In a little shop next-
door, the publican's wife was selling picturesque and
shoddy goods to two harassed Ruthenian women.

We slept in the hay. During the night one of the local
skinny cows calved below us. In the morning we went
back up into the mountains where I had lost a knife, a
keepsake, the day before. Beyond the forest's edge was
a grassy slope with a few small spruces and junipers. It
was so quiet you could hear the ringing of the dew, and
the rising of the orange sun seemed noisy. A large
eagle-owl on a tree watched me with an evil eye from
his freely rotating head. From the pasture to our right

and left, horses began to crowd in on us, two, three, seven of them. They stopped and watched me quietly from devoted black eyes. One went along with me. There was a pre-human tertiary silence, the kind that well-fed singers identify with happiness. That day we hoped to continue across the frontier. But there the glorious Red Army was already encamped. Signal flares raised the alarm and they opened fire on us with machine guns.

The reason we wanted to discover Sub-Carpathian Ruthenia was Ivan Olbracht.

Ivan Olbracht (1882–1952), story-teller, novelist and journalist, first brought Sub-Carpathian Ruthenia into Czech awareness through his novel *Nikola Šuhaj, the Robber*, published in 1933. Coincidentally, the same year saw the publication of another influential book based on a Ruthenian theme, Karel Čapek's *Hordubal*. There were a few more Czech literary figures who found themselves in Sub-Carpathian Ruthenia in the 1930s, either as officials or for punishment or as enchanted pilgrims. From then on, Sub-Carpathia began growing into something that used to be a Czechoslovak identity. But that Czechoslovak identity is now gone; it ended for ever with the murder of the Jews, the severing of Sub-Carpathian Ruthenia in 1945 and the establishment of an independent Slovakia in 1993.

Yet this poor, forgotten and starved eastern tip of our republic did provide our writers with the stimulus for two important novels. Irritated by the aridity and staleness of western subjects, by the whipped-up barrenness of current Czech material, Olbracht and Čapek searched in the east and found something fresh, fragrant, colourful and at the same time archaic, exotic and unrepeatable. A pity only that these intoxicating flowers grow in a graveyard: in the graveyard of a dying people threatened by hunger, police rifles and proletarianisation. You worthy writers, has it occurred to you that you are collecting botanical specimens in a graveyard? And that the butterfly you have caught and mounted with the pin of your poetic skill resembles a death's head?

This would be doubly true of Olbracht's later stories about the Sub-Carpathian Jews. By the time he was in his thirties, Olbracht, classified as a critical, or even a socialist realist, already had a number of 'vagabond stories' behind him: *The Wicked Loners* (1913), a somewhat Freudian soul-searching novel called *The Darkest Prison* (1916), and a fictional analysis of the role of the individual in society, *The Strange Friendship of the Actor Jesenius* (1919). He was a well-known author, predestined to be a socialist friend of the USSR thanks to his journalistic *Pictures from Contemporary Russia* (1920–1).

Whereas Čapek was the exponent of democratic thought and Czech pragmatic humanism, Olbracht was, from the outset, an explicitly socialist writer and journalist. I remember that in our middle-class family there was talk of Čapek whenever we discussed literature, whereas the name of Olbracht was only mentioned when the conversation turned to politics. While Čapek was a frequent visitor to the philosopher-president of Czechoslovakia, Tomás Garrigue Masaryk, in Prague

Castle, Olbracht was twice imprisoned for representing a Communist threat to democracy. He wrote about this experience in his accusatory book, *Mirror with Bars* (1930). Olbracht's views, like those of many other leading writers, were changed – yet not fundamentally shaken – by his expulsion from the Communist Party in 1929.

The previous year he had published his weighty and devotedly stereotyped proletarian novel, *Anna, the Proletarian*. However, by then he had realised that what really mattered was not the proletariat but the politburo. Olbracht was one of a group of seven socialist writers who were beginning to divorce the artistic avant-garde from party politics and who wanted to get beyond the 'political witch-hunts' as the illusions of the 1920s evaporated. Something like an existentialist anxiety about the economic situation and the threat to the very existence of Czechoslovakia descended on their souls. This group of seven also included Jaroslav Seifert.

During the war Olbracht again became a member of an underground Communist group, and after 1945 he was a member of the Central Committee of the Communist Party of Czechoslovakia. He held senior posts in radio and later in the Orwellian Ministry of Information. Yet socialist writers of Olbracht's type were a much greater thorn in the flesh of the party bosses and dogmatists than those labelled 'bourgeois writers'.

Čapek's and Olbracht's works shared a curious fate. They were never totally removed from literary history or from the school books, as happened to so many others over the past sixty years. After the war the works of both writers became classics of Czech literature, prescribed school texts and obligatory items in anyone's personal library, whether large or small. Čapek was shielded from the hostility of the Communist regime by the interest of Soviet scholarship. Following the collapse of Communism, Olbracht's position was saved precisely by the works of his Sub-Carpathian period. To be a set school book may be a gloomy fate, but it is the only way to take root in the mental software of today's teenagers as they sit at their computers absorbing virtual reality.

After 1929 Olbracht returned to Sub-Carpathian Ruthenia and its social problems, into which he now also projected his earlier stereotype of rebellion, liberation and Messianic faith. He had been prepared for this by his years in Vienna (1909–15): as a social democrat journalist he had made the acquaintance of a man who knew Sub-Carpathia and who also arranged for his subsequent sojourn there.

Olbracht arrived in Volové in 1931 and later went to Koločava, the place where the real Nikola Šuhaj had lived (and continued to live, in the memory of the local old women). He wrote articles for newspapers and studied the region and its people with a thoroughness characteristic of great writers. After two years, by then an expert on Sub-Carpathian Ruthenia, he wrote the screenplay for the film *Maria, the Unfaithful Wife*. He directed the film jointly with Vladislav Vancura, a powerful Czech novelist and linguistic innovator.

After five years, Olbracht returned from Sub-Carpathia, having published not only *Nikola Šuhaj*, but also a book of studies of the region (*Mountains and Centuries*). He brought with him the manuscript drafts of three stories which he developed into a book entitled *Valley of Exile*. The book was first published in 1937 and by 1983 had already been reprinted fourteen times. It consisted of two anecdotal stories, *The Miracle of Julka* and *The Affair of the Mikvah*, and the main long short story, almost a novella, *The Sorrowful Eyes of Hannah Karajich*. Although some of the characters appear unchanged throughout the book and although its three parts support each other within the framework of Sub-Carpathian reality, the story of *Hannah Karajich* speaks for itself. Here the universal human problem far transcends folklore. These are not cosy, poignant little incidents, or the literary equivalent of *Fiddler on the Roof*. Here is a drama of rebellion and the accomplished tragedy of liberation without catharsis, something that was fundamental for Olbracht the writer.

What makes the stories in *Valley of Exile* especially strange is that Olbracht focuses entirely on the Hasidic Jews. Czech tourists only pop up here and there, Czech towns are only casually visited, the Czechoslovak gendarmes only arrive just in time and the Ruthenians stand behind their fences like a silent chorus. There are but two *dramatis personae*: the Hasidim and the mountains. Why should the Czech novelist Olbracht concentrate so much on the Jews? Was it only because of their social interest, so different from the Jewish tradition of Vienna or Prague and from Czech cultural history? Was it irritation with 'the aridity and staleness of western subjects'? Was it an artistic or some other kind of premonition of the Jewish tragedy during the war?

It was none of these. It was an entirely personal choice. Olbracht was half-Jewish: his mother came from a wealthy Czech Jewish family. His father was a Czech writer and lawyer, called Zeman, who had taken the *nom de plume* of Antal Stašek. Olbracht followed him in adopting a pseudonym. But, in a manner of speaking, he retained his mother in his soul. He followed and quoted from Jewish literature and when, in the early 1930s, he began translating from German he chose almost exclusively books connected with Jewish destinies and the works of Jewish authors who were fleeing from the Nazi catastrophe. He translated Jakob Wassermann's *Road to Golgotha* (1931), Lion Feuchtwanger's *Jewish War* and, together with his first partner Helena Malírová, he began translating and publishing Thomas Mann's *Joseph and His Brothers* (1934, 1937). At the same time he discovered those poor wretches, the Sub-Carpathian Jews, who both appealed to his social conscience and struck a deep personal chord.

'Many of us,' a well-known Slovak director told me recently, 'discover in ourselves our Jewish roots' – probably not as a Messianic syndrome or orthodox obstinacy, but as a commitment arising from a European history of suffering, injustice and survival. Without any particular search among my own ancestors I can confirm from my own, probably non-Jewish, position that this is a syndrome which forms part of Czech cultural awareness or self-knowledge. Needless to say, it does not form part of Czech primitive tavern hooliganism, which thinks of Jews being too clever to share the fate of Czech plebeians.

The mere historical fact of the Galician and Sub-Carpathian Jews was, or could have been, an argument against the Czech 'tradition' of Jewish plutocrats, Jewish Bolsheviks and even the *Feldkurat* Katz types, as created by Jaroslav Hašek, author of *The Good Soldier Svejk*. In this respect Olbracht's triptych in the *Valley of Exile* was a fundamental cultural act. But it is also Olbracht's deeply personal testimony.

Ivan Olbracht's mother was the hidden prototype of Hannah Karajich, originally known by her Yiddish names as Hanele Shafar. In his postscript to the latest Czech edition of *Valley of Exile,* the literary critic Miloš Pohorský quotes from a letter written by Olbracht's mother, née Schönfeldová, to her future husband Antonín Zeman, alias Antal Stašek: 'Last night I asked myself what it could possibly be that might divide our souls. I put the question to myself and my heart replied: not circumstances, not people, no power on earth, provided his heart is as strong as yours. Then I put the question to you and my inflamed fantasy let me hear an answer that nearly drove me to despair. I heard you say: a Jewess! Tell me, oh tell me that this is not so, that you are willing to make just one sacrifice when I want to give my life for you – that you will not turn away because in name I belong to another faith, that you will take it as the truth when I tell you: my religion, my faith are you!'

In *The Sorrowful Eyes* the mother of Ivo Karajich, originally 'from a great line, of the name Cohen', now a disbeliever and apostate from Judaism, explains why her son wants to marry a girl from an orthodox Jewish family: 'It is his blood calling him. In spite of all his funeral orations and all his anti-Jewish talk!' And of Hanele Shafar's eyes, which are the key metaphor of the whole story, she says: 'They are rather sad. Our poets call it the sorrow of thousands of years. I'm afraid your eyes will become even sadder. Do you know what the eyes of the first generation look like? I mean the first generation to leave the Jewish faith and way of life. The people who throw all the ugly and the beautiful fairy-tales on the rubbish heap . . . I have always found their eyes moving. There is much more than the sorrow of thousands of years in them. There is an uneasiness, a strange bitterness, an eternal anxiety, perhaps the fear of hurting those we have left, or those who have not yet accepted us . . .'

I do not know what eyes Mrs Zemanová-Schönfeldová had. But I suspect that was how Ivan Olbracht came to the subject of the sorrowful eyes of Hannah Karajich. And thus it is that in *The Sorrowful Eyes of Hannah Karajich* the author speaks with profound feeling of the Jewish problem at all levels. I, at least, have never met a Czech Jew who would have regarded Olbracht's mirror as crooked. Such a judgement would, I believe, be due to an optical fault in a person's vision, remote in time and space. The tragedy of Hanele's parents, who lose their daughter, is already contained in the conciseness and restraint of his style, without interjections, without bombast, without wilfulness. It is conveyed simply in his account of behaviour, which is reminiscent of Lot whom Jahve did not spare at the destruction of Sodom.

Perhaps Olbracht failed to catch faithfully that general Hasidic trend towards exaltation rather than scholarly ostentation. But he certainly caught the bitter mentality of a people abandoned by everyone except the Messiah who will not and will not come. And he caught the human dimension of the disaster of Hanele's final departure from her home, 'Goodbye Father, Goodbye Mother.' Today I see in that scene something that took place ten thousand times on the ramp at Auschwitz. After that poetry can no longer be what it was before. Not even death can be what it was before.

The narrative method which began to make its appearance in Czech prose writing in the 1930s and which Olbracht practised with great consistency proves highly successful in this departure scene, in the sequence of persuasion and non-persuasion which precedes it, and finally in Karajich's clash with the Jewish crowd. This scene, too, Olbracht had repeatedly and thoroughly reworked, though it may seem as if it had written itself. We find here a seamless transition between the author's stance and that of his characters, with their motivations and their persistent myths. At times the author even views the action with a delicately disapproving irony. The characters then reveal themselves in a sophisticated form of inner monologue which is not questioned by the author but links up sharply with his depiction of the scene and authorial comment.

Thus the role of the governor Egan, who 'burdened the Jews with inordinate taxes', is presented by an objective account of his actions, although the language then blends into the diction of the Hasidim: 'The Lord had destroyed Egan, but allowed the man's laws to survive him that His people might be turned aside from the piling up of wealth, to remind His people of the duty of humility, and to bring them back to their mission in exile.' Or in the description of Hanele's sufferings: 'A fortnight later Hanele returned home . . . What's to be done with her, Mother? There are four who are dead while still alive: the poor, the blind, the leper, and the one who is childless. It looked as though Hanele would be doubly dead . . . '

This switching of voices is a kind of authorial licence and strengthens the impression of authenticity. The resulting effect, admittedly, is a certain scarcely surmountable and irresolvable sadness, in spite of an occasional gentle smile by the author. Miloš Pohorský believes that the 'authorial subject' linking all the components of the work is a sadness, which 'persists even at the bottom of narrative comedy and irony'. 'A sadness accompanying a longing for fulfilment in personal life . . . is permanently perceptible in Olbracht's prose as an undertone of his historical optimism and his view on life.'

A second characteristic, difficult to render in translation, is the language used by Olbracht and which for us today has the strange charm of pre-war Czech interlaced with Hebrew expressions and with Yiddish, that mixture of Hebrew, High German and local elements. Even a Czech reader now experiences the language of *The Sorrowful Eyes* as a transgression, albeit a comprehensible transgression, of his linguistic horizon, as a language pointing backwards and, at the same time, bringing the past into the present. It is the language of an authentic myth in which he involuntarily participates, even though Olbracht may be just as irretrievably remote from him as the Sub-Carpathian Jews. Its emotionality is exceedingly close to him, if only because he involuntarily experiences something like a short circuit into the Holocaust and its consequences.

The reader of *The Sorrowful Eyes of Hannah Karajich* cannot fail to feel that Hannah has freed herself from the myth and liberated herself from the hopelessness of the oppressive Carpathian village – but that she will also regret this for the rest of her life.

In our present-day context of demonstrative and impertinent post-modernism I consider any literature in which someone is hoping for liberation, or for any other civic ideal, and in which anybody feels sorry for anything at all, as the light at the end, or indeed at the beginning, of the tunnel. I share with Olbracht the conviction that even dark things should be talked about clearly. Literature, in the interest of its own survival, must turn to the people and not to some sour-faced intellectuals who wear sunglasses even in the black of night.

After 1945, the machine guns of the glorious Red Army prevented Ivan Olbracht from discovering what had become of his Polana, in reality probably Koločava.

Perhaps only that one Jew was left in Ruský Potok; he walked with his horse down with me from the upland pasture. The dark waters of time have closed over the Hasidim. A double barrier has come down between the Czech remnant of Czechoslovakia and the Ruthenian tip of the Ukraine, which belongs neither here nor there. One might think that Ivan Olbracht would have a few streets and a youth hostel named after him, but that nobody gives a damn about his Sub-Carpathia.

One would be wrong to think so. Olbracht's region is appearing once more in the imaginative life of the Czech Republic. The first two stories from *Valley of Exile* were made into a film in 1996, directed by Zeno Dostál, although unfortunately this portrayed the Jews rather as Hollywood romanticises Sioux and Hopi Indians. At present, one of our best directors, Karel Kachyně, is preparing to film *The Sorrowful Eyes of Hannah Karajich*. We must hope that he will get closer to the true spirit of those sorrowful eyes and the ruin of the house of Shafar.

More importantly, we find that we still have among us enough people who are sorry about something or other. In the 1990s, a Society of Friends of Sub-Carpathian Ruthenia was founded under the chairmanship of the poet Jaromír Hořec, who was born there into the family of a Czech forestry official. The society, now with 1,200 members, not only concerns itself with cultural nostalgia, lectures and publications, it also organises regular consignments of humanitarian aid for a country which today has neither a Messiah nor bandages, and which has to be reached through Slovakia.

Introduction

Even negotiations with the Slovak and Ukrainian customs officials turn into a cabbalistic experience. Why do they subject themselves to it? I believe that they are doing so also in Olbracht's name.

Sorrowful eyes are fashionable nowadays. But only those Sub-Carpathian ones have their own profound justification.

Miroslav Holub

Miroslav Holub sent this text to us just a couple of days before his untimely death. It therefore unwittingly acquires the character of a literary testament. It has been translated into English by his long-time friend and collaborator, Ewald Osers, and I have edited it for this edition.

Timothy Garton Ash

The Sorrowful Eyes
of Hannah Karajich

The eyes of Hannah Karajich, once the most beautiful eyes in all Polana,* almond-shaped eyes incredibly wide and dark, so deep they made your head swim, their long lashes softening to sweetness, whose gleam no man's heart could bear unveiled – the most wonderful eyes in the whole countryside have grown sorrowful, and sorrowful will they remain until the moment when her dear Ivo (God grant that it be he!) gently weights them down with a silver coin. And it would seem highly probable that the children of Hannah Karajich will inherit the strange gleam of those deep eyes.

'Ivo Karajich and his wife Hanichka, née Shaffer, have pleasure in announcing . . .'

Lord! How strange it sounds!

How *goy** it sounds! How different it looks spelt that way,* and how right the wise and learned men are when they say: 'Jewry is a chain! Shake but a link and the whole will fall apart! Double a letter or take away a vowel, and all is destroyed!'

Hannah Karajich remembers the family wealth only as a legend, and she can hardly remember Grandfather Abraham at all. All she knows is that her eldest sister

3

Etelka had a dowry of two hundred thousand pre-war crowns, and that Bálinka's dowry was still good enough for a fur merchant in Mukachevo* to marry her. There was nothing left for the youngest daughter, Hannah, whom they called Hanele.* Yet it had been great wealth, and Grandfather had been famed among the famous, the great Abraham Shafar of Polana, who used to sit with Count Palugyay and Pálfy and Berceny* in Budapest, drinking expensive liqueurs (not wine, oh dear, no! that was not permissible, because the Christians use wine for their ritual magic) and playing cards with them for ducats. What was the little inn and village shop now, you could carry it off lock, stock and barrel in three baskets on your back; and what was the great big house with its dilapidated farm buildings, the balcony falling into disrepair, boards working loose in the floors and clattering whenever you made a false step; what was all that compared to what the place was like in Grandfather's time? Almost half the land in Polana had belonged to Grandfather Abraham, and more than half the villagers' communal tract of forest: he had owned a quarry; seven of the Ruthenian* peasant cottages had been his property and all three mills on the stream and the brooks. Ah, those mills! Delightful little mills that Hannah Karajich will never forget if she lives to be a hundred. Each of them drove a beetle, and the wooden hammers falling on the sheep's wool with a dull thud kept up a strange rhythm that she could hear only at night, when everything was still, a strange night song that can no longer be heard anywhere in the world. When Hanele was a little child the sound of the mills lulled her to sleep, their music crept into her girlhood dreams, and the rhythm of thudding blows deadened by sheep's wool, handed on from one mill to the next would certainly have become the rhythm of her adult life too, had not the night song of Polana been broken off so sharply and for ever.

Grandfather Abraham had been rich in other ways, too. He rented mountain pastures from His Lordship* and farmed them out to the Ruthenian peasants at a profit. His cattle were scattered far and wide in cottage sheds and winter byres, for the Lord blessed his flocks and his herds, and Grandfather used to put his heifers out to pasture with the peasants' cattle in summer and feed with them in winter, and the peasants then had the right to the milk and half the calves. Grandfather Abraham loaned money, too, fifty guilders* at a daily interest of ten hellers*, which was only raised if the Ruthenians happened to be finding cattle-running a profitable business, or if the loan was a large one borrowed only for a few days. Hannah Karajich, as if in a dream, and not sure whether she really remembers it or has heard others describe it, recalls mysterious financial negotiations in the little room behind the tap-room, whispered conversations with a peasant in a corner of the shop, Grandfather gazing sternly from beneath bushy brows as he slowly felt for his once-red pocket-book fastened with a strap. From a later time she remembers quite clearly rows of peasant carts filled with gravel from Grandfather's quarry, and men waiting in the inn for the order to start work; all Grandfather's debtors worked off their interest and sometimes even the whole debt, with their own hands and with their horses, in his fields or by laying gravel on the roads or repairing paths and bridges in the forests. There was no one who could compete with Shafar of Polana when it came to contracting for public works. And whatever money might be earned in the village by any other means, cutting timber or floating rafts down the river, it all came to rest sooner or later between the banknotes already tucked away in Grandfather's pocket-book fastened with a strap, or dropped with a tinkle through the holes cut in the wooden counters of the shop and the inn bar, once upon a time neatly squared but now worn smooth into round little hollows by the family's fingertips.

Where does money go to when it keeps on coming into the house (and the Lord be thanked, it's always trickling in even if it doesn't pour!) and the family pays out practically nothing except what goes in taxes? When the mud of the big farmyard is criss-crossed by the tracks of flocks of geese, ducks, turkeys and hens, when there is enough flour from your own mills, fruit and vegetables from your own garden and orchard, milk and meat from your own flocks and herds, and some to spare? When your cupboards are full of linen and crockery, and the silver candlesticks for the glory of the Sabbath supper have been inherited from your forefathers? And when even footwear costs no more than a bit of leather out of the shop, because old Leyzer Abrahamovich works off his interest with his cobbler's awl? Is it any wonder that the family wealth grows day by day?

M. Barth, biographer of the Governor, Edmond Egan,* the scourge of God and destroyer of every trace of Jewish prosperity in these parts, was apparently not interested in the people or the place concerned in the incident he describes, and gives no names. In fact, it took place in Polana and the hero was Abraham Shafar, then a man in his prime. As the much-feared Governor drove through the village with a couple of hunting cronies, Abraham Shafar came out in front of his house to meet him with his three youngest daughters, who were very beautiful and wore white muslin dresses with gathered frills on the skirt and sashes round their waists, one red, one white and one green. Their father was bold enough to take his stand in the middle of the road and spread his arms wide to bring the gig to a standstill. The youngest girl handed the all-powerful Governor a silver tray on which a glass of red, a glass of white and a glass of green liqueur were arranged to form the Hungarian tricolour, and since the Governor could hardly refuse refreshment offered in so patriotic a fashion by so lovely a maiden, Abraham Shafar waited for him to put the liquid to his lips and then drew near. He said; 'Will my most merciful master allow a humble Jew one single question?' And assuming two seconds of somewhat astonished silence to mean consent, he went on; 'My powerful and high-born master has a fishpond, and in it there are two kinds of fishes: a few large fat fishes that bring my master considerable profit every year, and many small, thin fishes, good for nothing, on which the fat fishes feed. It is rumoured that my master is now thinking of destroying the fat and highly profitable fishes, in order to give more opportunity to the little fishes that are good for nothing. An ignorant Jew of

Polana, who does not understand many things, does not understand this thing; and he humbly asks: Is my powerful and high-born master acting wisely?' Egan laughed heartily and nodded his head to the coachman, who whipped up the horses.

It is quite clear why Hanele could not remember the family riches but yet could remember her Grandfather. Wealth melts away unnoticed, trickles away through the fingers and is gone, so that except for those days when misfortune fell, in itself never enough to cause catastrophe, you cannot even say exactly when it disappeared. Though man dies suddenly, his departure is accompanied by emotions that cannot be forgotten, and religious observances that are moving and memorable. It is not only the death itself. It is not only the funeral and 'Lord, let Thy servant depart in peace!' the way *goyim* put their dead out of their lives. You must rend your garments, even if you do not take it literally, since in addition to things not of this world one must also remember the price of cloth, and both God and the deceased will be satisfied if you take a knife and make a little cut in the lapel of your coat or the hem of the women's dresses, and tear it just a little; for eight days you are commanded to sit barefoot on the bare ground and recite the prayers for the dead; it is fitting to have a picture made and hung on the wall, showing for tens of years ahead the days on which the day of commemoration of the dead will fall according to the Jewish calendar, when it will be your duty to treat the congregation in the synagogue to alcohol, to visit the grave and, in addition, to sit on the ground for *shiva*,* the week of mourning. God and the dead have both seen to it that they will not be forgotten; God for ever, and the dead as long as their near relatives are still alive.

These are not the only memories that remain with Hannah Karajich, never allowing her to forget her Grandfather. If we call the one terrible, what words can we find for the other, far more dreadful? It is the memory of the prayer the people of Israel recite as the dead body is carried out: no longer a human being, a brother, for his soul has gone to his Maker; but a human carcass, an unclean heap of stinking flesh already in the claws of demons tearing at it and devouring it. The memory of the pitiless, cruel, hated and a thousand times accursed prayer to the words of which the house of Israel casts out from its midst all that is unclean.

No; the day the coffin containing Grandfather's body was carried out of the house Hanele wept just as those around her did, but she paid no attention to the prayer, she did not know who was praying for what, she did not even understand the words, because girls are not taught the language of the Lord.* Yet it was to be her fate to hear this funeral prayer repeated in her own lifetime; and what was most terrible, to hear it repeated without a funeral, without anyone having died, at a moment when her own death would have come as a mercy and a liberation for Hannah. This took place when the soft rhythm of the Polana nights, the rhythm so lovingly offered for her whole life by the thudding hammers of Grandfather's mills, was broken off so sharply and for ever. . . And it was all due to the fateful repetition of this pitiless prayer that the most beautiful eyes in Polana have grown sorrowful, and that perhaps the eyes of Hannah's children will be sorrowful too.

Perhaps it really was Egan who was at the root of all their troubles – the Governor whose heart was filled with hate and who burdened the Jews with inordinate taxes, passed new laws preventing them from lending money to advantage and from buying up common land, and who, by setting up a network of credit and consumers' co-operatives, taught the villagers to spend their money elsewhere.

The Lord took His revenge on him before he left this earth. At twilight one evening, as he was climbing down from the gig he was driving, alone, on a deserted forest path, the Lord caused a bullet to issue from Egan's own gun. Next day they found the horse, still in harness, grazing peacefully in a ditch while a considerable distance away lay the dead body with a terrible wound in the belly. People blamed the crime on the Jews at the time, and they still do, to this day. Fools! As if the Lord were not mightier than men, and as if a Jew would ever commit murder! Yet who could blame Israel for praising the Lord over-joyfully that day, and declaring loudly that the measure of His chastisement had been filled? The Lord had destroyed Egan, but allowed the man's laws to survive him, that His people might be turned aside from the piling up of wealth, to remind His people of the duty of humility, and to bring them back to their mission in exile.

The Jew-hater was not responsible for everything, though. Grandfather may have been a bit to blame himself.

He started a legal case against Hersch Fuchs, the father of Solomon Fuchs, an ugly old Polish Jew who had turned up in Polana with his grown-up son, from God knows where in Galicia, and God only knows why. Hersch was practically a beggar, beneath everyone's notice, then he bettered himself a bit by marrying the aunt of Baynish Zisovich, a woman ten years his senior, and made his living as best he could: doing a day's work now and again on His Lordship's land, and doing the rounds of the cottages in the spring with wicker baskets on both arms and on his back, buying up eggs for the market – for Grandfather's money, naturally, at twenty per cent, and the loan was more an act of charity than a commercial transaction, for nobody else would have given Hershko credit at all. One day, later on, he came asking for a loan of eight thousand, appealing to Grandfather's religious duty of neighbourly charity (and if the words *al gemilut khasadim** are spoken between Jews, it is indeed a matter of great moment); he said he had the chance of a stretch of forest practically for nothing, he would be able to make a good deal, and his whole future depended on it. Who did 'Hershko' think he was. Even the Ruthenians called him that.* Who was he to go borrowing thousands of crowns? Grandfather shook his head. But Hershko came round day after day, begging, weeping, offering to give his oath before the Rabbi and *al gemilut khasadim* cropped up again – and in the end Abraham Shafar gave way. Hershko did not use Grandfather's eight thousand to buy a stretch of forest, but instead set up a little shop and tap-room . . . When Grandfather got news from the town about this new licence, he did not say a word; he just went as white as a sheet.

From then on Hersch Fuchs began to prosper ominously. He undercut prices, ignoring the common decencies observed among fellow-shopkeepers, luring customers away from the Shafars'. Every day he carried his head a bit higher, he began to dress decently; after Wolf died he bought the dead man's place in the synagogue – one of the most coveted – and respect for him mounted: *Mr* Hersch Fuchs.

Grandfather was a strange man. You would not have thought it, but he was incredibly ambitious. For years he held his tongue, accepting the agreed sums with which Hersch paid off his debt, and even passing the time of day with him; only his heart was eaten up by the thought of what he had brought about himself. One Saturday morning Hersch appeared in the synagogue in a new *tallith,** a wonderful *tallith* edged with silver and far more beautiful than the most valuable *tallith* hitherto known in Polana – Grandfather's. The congregation glanced first at one *tallith*, then at the other, first at Fuchs and then at Shafar – and then they smiled. That was when Grandfather went white for the second time. No, this was more than he could stand.

The next day he called in the whole of the loan. Take that! Under the sod with him! It was high time to put Mr Fuchs in his proper place. A filthy Polish Jew! Abraham Shafar? He would soon see who Shafar of Polana was! Then Hersch Fuchs contested the amount of the loan. Grandfather went to court over it. Hersch Fuchs retaliated with a charge of usury. Grandfather started litigation over Hersch's meadow, then over an orchard one of the peasants had given Fuchs the use of in surety for a loan, then over the right of way through Hersch's wife's yard. He betrayed to the Ruthenians the fact that they could not be prosecuted for debts incurred over the sale of liquor, and urged them to withhold payment from Hersch. That will teach you, you mangy cur! Under the sod with you!

It is unusual for a Jew to bear a grudge against a *goy*; he does not consider him his equal, he looks down on him, he may even scorn him. But when a Jew bears a grudge against a Jew, there is none more bitter. This one even extended beyond the grave, beyond the graves of both of them, for the lawsuits dragged on right through the war years and for a long time afterwards. It was left to the sons, Mr Solomon Fuchs and Hanele's father, Joseph Shafar, to bring them to an end with the same bitter hatred, for by then the sums involved were far too great for there to be any thought of reconciliation. The lawsuits cost a huge amount of money – to pay for lawyers and for witnesses. As long as Grandfather was alive he was always the one with more witnesses.

The war* was certainly to blame for much of this, though Father ought to take his share of the blame, too.

Grandfather was very old by then, and often sick, and spent a lot of time at prayer in his little room beyond the bar. He had long since married off the youngest of his six daughters with a dowry. A few months before war broke out he had settled with his Budapest son for what remained of his share of the estate, sold some of the land, and turned the running of the place over to Joseph,

Hanele's father. Father had always lived with Grandfather. He had been married for years and his children were growing up; Etelka was growing into a woman, Bálinka was going to school and Hanele had come into the world, she was just learning to crawl then. But Grandfather was still head of the family, and Father and Mother were only his underlings in the shop and the tap-room; Abraham Shafar would not allow his son to handle the bigger transactions. 'Ach, I'd rather see to that myself. You haven't got the lucky touch,' he used to say.

Is it fitting for a Jew to stand at a factory lathe if he hasn't even the faintest idea what a lathe is for? They were still wealthy, then; Grandfather had plenty of influential friends, and what was more important, he knew what addresses to send money to. A lot of money moved around, during those four years. All through the war Father was at his lathe in Budapest, turning out shrapnel and hand-grenades for the army. A lot of people were said to have made money during the war. Father couldn't. And Grandfather was getting old.

Then the war came to an end, or maybe it did not come to any end and it was only the papers that said so. Anyway, Father came home.

The terrible memory of Grandfather that haunts Hanele to this day dates from this time, a time she can still remember quite clearly. Worse than tales of ghosts and flaming corpses in abysses, it is a murky, embarrassing memory, all the more shameful because she will never be able to confide in her parents, her sisters, her friends, not even in her future husband.

What strange times those were! Whom did Polana*
belong to? Hungary? Rumania? The Bolsheviks? A
Ukrainian government was set up in Yasina. There were
even people who said the Czechs were going to take
over. It was a profitable business to smuggle tobacco in
those days, worth the moments of anxiety. In Rumania
it was six or seven times as cheap, and you could easily
pack a hundred thousand crowns' worth under the box
in the trap. If you could call it a frontier in those days,
it was to the frontier that Father used to go for his
Rumanian tobacco, to an inn on the edge of a certain
village. He would drive the trap in for the night and
leave before daylight with the goods.

One night great shouts were heard outside and someone started thundering on the inn door. The innkeeper
ran to open up. The military! Father was terrified. He
jumped out of bed, ran wildly about the room and then
crawled under the bed. It was an officer and two men.
They found the tobacco. It had not even been hidden
and was lying neatly packed in the lobby. They found
Father, too. They hauled him out, slapped his face and
beat him up. The officer got into Father's bed and the
men took turns to stand guard over him till morning.

Next morning they all got into the trap.

'What's your name, stinking Jew?'

'Joseph Shafar from Polana.'

'Get a move on! Up with you!'

And they set off. They were not going in the direction
of Polana, so they must be making for their headquarters
somewhere. One of the men was driving; he looked like
a gypsy. The other man sat by Father and the officer sat

15

alone on the comfortable seat, smoking one cigarette after another. The tobacco was stowed away under the box. The soldiers were armed with rifles. They drove along in silence for about half an hour. When they were five kilometres or so from a side road that would take them to Polana, Father said, as though he was talking to himself, or rather, as though he was addressing the air: 'The gentleman could do well out of this and I could do well, too.'

There was no reply. The lieutenant went on smoking and gazed stolidly over Father's shoulder at the landscape. They drove on and on, and it was quite a while before the man sitting by Father spoke: 'How much?'

'Ten thousand,' Father replied.

'When?'

'Straightaway, if we drive to Polana instead of to your headquarters.'

They said no more, but Father thought the lieutenant and the man at his side were exchanging glances. A little later the man said, as though he had thought better of it, 'That's not enough.'

'Fifteen,' Father hastily replied.

'Not enough, Jew!'

'I haven't got more than that at home.'

Nevertheless, when they reached the crossroads they turned off on to the track that led to Polana. It was late afternoon when they reached the village.

Father ordered Mother to produce the best dinner she could, sat the men down in the tap-room and led the lieutenant into the best room in the house. He paid him the promised sum, down to the last heller, gave him food and good wine, and was the soul of hospitality.

After dinner the lieutenant said he was bored.

'Would the gentleman like to play cards?'

The officer shook his head wearily and went to join his men in the tap-room. They had had their dinner and were now drinking cheap wine.

The lieutenant sat down with them. They went on drinking and Father went on filling their glasses. They struck up a song, and roared it out until the rafters shook. Then they started drinking spirits. Father took advantage of this propitious moment; unobserved he took their rifles off the hook, carried them into the stable on the far side of the farmyard, and hid them under the drinking trough.

He was glad they had taken to drinking spirits, for they would be drunk all the sooner and go to sleep, and all would be well. He was only upset because they were sitting in the tap-room. All his attempts to draw them into the neighbouring room failed.

'Get out of the way,' the men swung their arms at him, and carried on making their noise.

He was upset by what Mother had anxiously whispered to him in the kitchen: she had not seen them coming in time, and so had not managed to get Etelka out of the house. She had hastily pushed her into the little room where Grandfather lay in bed. The only way out of this room was through the tap-room, and since Grandfather's windows were barred, Etelka could not escape that way either. Yankel the carter, whom Mother had sent to look for the two smaller girls, had found

Hanele and Bálinka on the street and taken them to *beder** Kahan's house. Mother was dreadfully anxious.

The men were soon drunk, and the lieutenant in particular looked as though he would not hold out much longer; he could not stop himself laughing, and did not seem to be used to the strong spirits he was pouring down his throat like water. Perhaps nothing would happen after all, pray God! The men forced the Jew to drink a toast to king and country and the Christian religion, and Father complied with a polite smile, knowing that it did not count if in your mind you thought the opposite. Anyway, it was only water he was pouring into his own glass.

Soon the lieutenant needed to go outside; his feet kept tying themselves in knots, and that seemed to afford him great amusement.

The two men were singing at the tops of their voices, arms around one another's shoulders. Father shut and bolted the door leading from the tap-room into the street.

At that moment loud laughter announced the lieutenant's return. He stumbled over the threshold, spread his arms wide in the open doorway, and his laughter grew to a yell of delight; 'There's a beauty in the house! A wonderful beauty! I've got to have a look at her. Bring her in here!'

From the yard he must have caught a glimpse of Etelka, venturing carelessly too close to the window.

Father was terrified, but he did not show it. 'The gentleman is joking.'

'No!' yelled the lieutenant, glaring.

'The gentleman must have imagined it. A beauty? What sort of a beauty? Where could that be, now?' And he smiled.

'No!' the lieutenant roared as though he was in the barracks' yard.

Mother rushed in from the kitchen, pale with terror. She caught at the officer's sleeve, stroking his arm and pleading in a trembling voice:

'No, no, no, there's nobody here at all, sir, of course there isn't . . .'

'There is!' the officer yelled back.

'I swear to you,' Mother cried. 'I swear by everything I hold dear in this world, I swear by my own life and that of my children!' She was giving herself away, being so upset, Father tried to drag her away from the lieutenant. 'No, no, there isn't anyone here, you can believe me.'

The officer seemed to have sobered up all of a sudden. He stood erect, his eyes blazing more with injured pride than with intoxication, and his words came in a strangely firm voice: 'I am not going to swear by anything, but I give you my word of honour as an officer that not a hair of the girl's head will be harmed. I have got to see her! I will kiss her hand gallantly and let her go her way. Bring her in here!' It was only the difficulty he had to get the word 'gallantly' straight that betrayed his drunkenness.

'No,' Mother was screaming again and swearing by everything she held dear.

The officer stopped paying any attention to her. His eyes were getting wilder and wilder. Suddenly his face

19

darkened. Turning to his men he stretched out his hand towards the door to Grandfather's room. 'In there! Break down that door!'

The men glanced round the walls of the room, but not seeing their weapons anywhere they rushed at the door unarmed.

'There's a man with smallpox in there! You'll get it and die!' Mother screamed desperately.

A blow on the face knocked her to the ground. Father was sent reeling into a corner. Then they ran at the door with their shoulders. Once. And then again. The wood cracked.

Suddenly the door opened inwards and Etelka dashed out, squealing fearfully, slipped under the men's arms and out through the kitchen to the farmyard.

It took the men a full two seconds to realise what had happened. Then all three set off after her.

Father stood in the middle of the bar, holding his head in his hands, but Mother still had the strength to run through the kitchen and the parlour to the window. There she saw Etelka dash across the orchard, slip through a gap where the crab-apple had been cut down, and run down to the brook. The men did not know their way about; when they got into the garden and over to the fence they lost time trying to climb it and then did not know which way to turn.

'Ach!' Mother gave a sigh of relief; she dropped into a chair and let her head drop on her hands on the table. 'Now let it come.'

It came, all right. The soldiers were infuriated when they got back. They began smashing up the tap-room.

The oil lamps hanging from the ceiling were the first victims, then they picked up chairs and smashed the glasses on the bar; then they started on the windows. The glass tinkled as it splintered down on to the balcony outside.

Father pushed Mother out of the house and went and hid himself in the farmyard; now and again he screwed up courage to step along the balcony and look cautiously through the windows with their three-cornered splinters of glass still holding in the frames, to watch the work of destruction going on inside.

They smashed the place to bits. Glasses, bottles, demijohns, chairs; splinters of wood and glass. They had overturned the bar counter. One of the soldiers was banging on the table with the stump of a chairleg and the blows resounded like shots. The other, the one who had driven the trap that morning and looked like a gypsy, was trying to kick the stove to pieces, but he could not get his heels high enough to kick it above the brick foundation, and staggered back after each attempt. The lieutenant was sitting cross-legged on the table, with bottles of spirits all round him (oh, how carefully they carried those bottles across the room to him!), shouting and howling with laughter and egging the men on.

Father wrung his hands. Would they start pillaging the house as well? Would they get into the other rooms? So far the idea had not occurred to them.

The gypsy had thought up a plan. He left off his vain jumping up and down and went to fetch an empty fifty-gallon cask. With all his strength he struck at the stove with the cask, and brought it down with a crash. A swarming pillar of soot rose from the rubble towards the ceiling and spread slowly through the room. The men were covered in it. The lieutenant's laughter turned to wild shrieks, he lay down and rolled about on the table (two bottles fell to the floor and broke), neighing and howling with mirth.

This was the moment Father had been waiting for. Staggering and stumbling and throwing his arms about, he reeled into the room with broken cries that were meant to resemble the tunes the men were roaring. Holding a glass of spirits in his hand, he began dancing among the desolation. Before long he was as black from the soot as they were, laughing and shrieking, crouching down and jerking his legs about like a puppet. He let the officer hurl a full glass in his face, he let the soldiers kick him and pull his sidecurls, still short from being cut off in the war, and let them push him about at will.

Then he took up his stand in the middle of the room and began toasting the king.

Praised be the name of the Lord! The gypsy fell for the trick. He seized a large bottle and drank great swigs from it. The others were not to be outdone. Father hurried into the kitchen for fresh glasses and kept filling them up.

From the kitchen window he caught sight of the women servants coming back from the fields, crossing themselves agitatedly. He turned them away, brought an oil lamp to light the bar, and closed the shutters across the smashed windows.

The toasts came thick and fast now. King and country and the army, bottoms up, spirits and spirits and more spirits. Father managed to keep going in that wild orgy of excitement.

The first to drop was the lieutenant – without warning, as if felled by a blow.

One of the other two was not long in following. He wanted to go outside but could not find the door, and now sat there on the floor in all the mess, his back propped against the iron door leading on to the street and his eyes, glassed over, staring sightless in front of him.

Father did not know what to do with the gypsy; he was like a bottomless pit. He sat there shouting his head off, and when he felt a touch he started trying to jump in the air again. Father called Yankel the carter in from the yard. Yankel got behind the gypsy and squeezed the man's jaws open. 'Long live His Majesty!' yelled Father wildly, and poured a large glass of methylated spirits into the open mouth. The gypsy's eyes dilated and he looked as though he was gasping for breath. For a few moments he sat on staring glassy-eyed, and then fell to the floor.

'Just a minute, one more minute, Mother,' Father called to his wife who was knocking impatiently on the shutters.

Then he staggered out into the farmyard and let Mother lead him to the well: there he drank in great gulps, rubbed the soot on his face with cold water, and let her lead him into the orchard to get a breath of fresh air and listen to her commiserations.

This was the moment when Hanele, who was not yet six, perhaps feeling the call of bedtime, slipped away from her sister and the *beder*'s children; unobserved, she trotted away from the Kahans' in the direction of home.

Why was the shop and the tap-room closed, and why were the shutters up so early?

She climbed the three millstones that served as steps up to the balcony, rounded the corner of the house and stood on tiptoe to squint through the gap where one of the shutters did not fit properly.

Two black men? . . . Two dead soldiers? . . . There might be three of them, because she could just see another pair of boots . . . She saw it all – or at least, a great deal too much.

Grandfather came shambling in on unsteady feet, wearing nothing but a nightshirt. His head was bald, his white sidecurls hung limply by his ears, and the sparse beard lying on his chest was yellowing with age. Grandfather stood there looking at the soldiers, then realising which of them was the officer, he tottered over to him. For a long time he stood looking down at the body, and the black eyes burning in the pale face, beneath shaggy brows like windswept tufts of grass, were terrible. Then he moved his feet a little apart.

No! . . . What was happening?

Grandfather was making water on the officer . . . sprinkling the blackened face . . . drenching the uniform . . .

No, Hanele could not understand what was happening; and it seems she will never realise the full implica-

24

tions of what Grandfather was doing then. It was not pouring scorn on mortal man. It was not revenge. What Hanele witnessed was something worse than murder.

Food itself, however strictly the ritual of preparation is adhered to, is an unclean thing, and a man who wishes to be strong in spirit should not consume much food. It contains unclean substances that are harmful to man, undermining his strength and above all the strength of his spirit, making it weak. The water passed by man draws all these impurities into itself; it is the essence of all that is unclean, the most unclean of all unclean things. A man on whom its drops fall ceases to be a man. Never again will he be capable of spiritual acts, his strength will ebb away and his will be sapped until he becomes for ever a phantom in the likeness of a man, a scrap of dirty cloth blown hither and thither in the wind. That is what is written in medieval Talmudic texts long since withdrawn from circulation: Jeshua Hanocri, seeking his own greater glory, stole into the Temple in Jerusalem and carried off *Shem ha-Meforash*, the parchment on which was inscribed the true name of God that no man may know; and having sewn it into a wound on his bosom, began to perform miracles through its power. Then the council of the elders came together, wrathful that the people should be thus deceived and even wise men led astray, and chose from their midst the pious Rabbi Jehuda; the Name of God was placed in a wound on his bosom, too, and Rabbi Jehuda went everywhere that Jeshua went, and performed all the miracles he performed. One day Jeshua rose up towards Heaven; Rabbi Jehuda rose even higher, above his head, and 'poured himself out' upon the other. At that very moment the True Name of God lost its power, Jeshua Hanocri fell headlong to the ground and was taken prisoner and executed.

That was what Grandfather was doing to the soldier. To the man who had poured scorn on the name of Israel, who had destroyed Jewish property, who had sought to dishonour a grand-daughter of Abraham Shafar.

He stood erect in the yellow light of the oil lamp, white-clad, white with age and sickness, and all the life in him was flowing through those gleaming black eyes beneath the tufted eyebrows. Then Grandfather began to sing, in a sad minor key, a mystic oriental melody that, rising as it were from a spell laid five thousand years ago, seemed to be calling forth from pasture lands and deserts the underground forces that had destroyed the Amalekites, the Midianites and the Philistines, that had wiped from the face of the earth the Romans, Babylon and Egypt, done Onan to death, and Korah, and Dathan and Abiram his brother, and Tola, and whomsoever wished ill to the people of Israel and their God. Grandfather, all trace of trembling old age forgotten, stood over the unconscious soldier and sang, ponderously, word by word and syllable by syllable, the terrible Talmudic curse;

'*Yey, hey regel shelkho tis-khabesh!* May thy blood dry up in thy veins and thy limbs lose their strength and fail thee; may thy thoughts be dulled and thy anger of no avail! For such is the reward of evil and thou shalt no longer have power to do the evil that thou hast prepared for us, the people of Israel. May the Lord thus punish thee! Amen.'

At this point Hanele dropped from tiptoe to normal stance, dashed along the balcony and down the steps into the yard crying despairingly in the darkness: 'Mammy, Mammy, Mammy!'

Mother hurried up from the orchard. 'Why aren't you at the *beder*'s, like I told you?' and vented her distress with a smack on the child's bottom.

No, Hanele said not a word of what she had seen. Later she simply lay in bed in the dark, terrified, her eyes wide and staring.

Meanwhile Father and Yankel had carried the lieutenant into another room, washed him and laid him in a white bed; Father put the officer's money and possessions in a neat pile on the bedside table and handed the uniform to Yankel: 'Take this round to Yakubovich's right away. Pinches has got to get it clean and wash and iron it. By morning it's got to look like new even if he has to work all night. You start polishing those boots of his until you can see your face in them.'

When Yankel got back from his errand to Yakubovich's, the two of them went into the bar. Father took the men by the feet and Yankel by the head, and one after the other they flung them down from the balcony into the dog-muck by the dung-heap. Not until morning did Yankel drag them both into the stable out of sight.

The men slept all night and all day and the next night too, and they had to throw a pan of water over the gypsy to bring him round even then. On Thursday morning the officer, pale-faced in his well-ironed uniform and shining polished boots, walked back and forth in the kitchen. He sounded ill-humoured as he asked: 'Today's Wednesday, isn't it?'

'What else could it be, Your Honour?'

'Weren't we a bit . . . you know . . . last night?'

'Not at all, sir, just a bit merry, that's all,' Father smiled politely and rubbed his hands.

Yankel harnessed the horse and the trap drove off.

On the seat, smoking one cigarette after another, sat what had once been a man, now a human phantom with no strength and no will, rendered harmless from now on, he would reel through life blind and helpless, however long that life might be.

Nobody knows what the Lord has planned for the people of Israel living in this land, or who is to rule over them.

In the beginning there were the Hungarians. Then came the Russians, then the Germans, then the Rumanians. And now the Czechs had moved in. The only way to tell the difference, in Polana, was by looking at the uniform caps of the police and the excise men.

Family fortunes melted away just the same, whoever was in power. The Czechs issued a regulation to the effect that Hungarian money was no longer to be used in private business transactions; only Czechoslovak currency was valid. Up to a given date, however, the authorities were prepared to exchange at the rate of a hundred Czechoslovak crowns for a hundred Hungarian.

It was a terrible time and desperate decisions had to be made. The Hungarians were already declaring that when they came back they were not going to exchange Hungarian for Czechoslovak crowns, and anyone whose wealth was in Czechoslovak currency would lose it. The Czechs declared that they would exchange money only up to a certain date, after which the Hungarian money would be valueless. Which was the safer bet, Hungary or Czechoslovakia? What could a poor Jew of Polana know about international intrigue, conflicting interests and rival monopolies, about the views of the kings of England and Italy, and of the presidents of France and Germany, and what they were likely to agree on in the end? What a grim joke, to confront him with such a dilemma. You might as well say to a man: Put everything you've got on one of two cards, the white or the black. There's no chance of winning; you can only lose everything, but you must make your choice, unhappy gambler . . . Will the Hungarians come back, or won't they? Shall I change that money, or not?

Money! The most precious form of property in the world. Just as important as health or family. 'There are four who are dead while yet alive,' says the Talmud: 'the poor man, the blind, the leper and the man who is childless.' But to be poor is worst of all. Only a simpleton thinks money is a means to an end, and that if he has got money it is for spending on maize flour, or spirits, or a string of glass beads for his wife. Money is the proof of success in life, the outward and visible sign of the Lord's favour. All the beauty and power of life is gathered together in those discs of metal and those blue-tinted pieces of paper: they are the things of the Lord. It would be wrong to waste them.

Father went to consult Grandfather in his little room. The old man was very weak, and hardly ever left his room or his bed. Grandfather shrugged his shoulders. He wrinkled his left nostril and half-closed his left eye. The bony white hand lying on the cover turned palm upwards and then back again: this way, or that?

'It's hard to say. We need to find out more about it. What can I do, these days? . . . 100:100 . . . that doesn't tell us anything. If it was 100:90 or 100:110, it would be easier to guess whether they really felt sure of themselves or were just trying to throw dust in our eyes. What you need here is the lucky touch . . . The best thing, of course, would be to get rid of ready money and buy gold, dollars, sterling, land, anything you can. But everybody's wiser nowadays and where will you find anybody willing to sell? . . . Buy what you can, pay everything you owe . . . then perhaps you'd better wait and see, as long as there's still time. If you want to be really prudent, change half the money. You'll lose half, anyway.'

This idea quite appealed to Father but Mother wept when they went to bed that night. 'You want to throw away half our money? All that wealth? Is that what we've worked our fingers to the bone for? No, No! Things will go on just as they were before; we've had Russians and Germans here in the past, Rumanians and Czechs. None of them will stay for ever, you'll see I'm right. Don't change the money!'

If you have never had any money of your own you cannot imagine how hard a decision like this can be. The red or the black? The right or the left? Deep in thought Father walked about Polana, not even aware of people speaking to him, while the village cared nothing for his worries. They were not interested, it did not concern them. It only concerned the Shafars and the Fuchs family.

What did Hersch and Solomon Fuchs think about it? Ever since the cases had been dragged through the courts, long ago, all contact between the Shafars and the Fuchs family had been severed; they did not even greet one another in the street. But Father could see that Solomon was prospering in everything he did, that he was flourishing, and he felt the other man must be very clever. Fuchs had his contacts among the new Czechoslovak authorities; the new powers-that-be lent him their favour, and he was sure to have inside information and know more than the others.

'What does Solomon Fuchs say?' He put the question to Mordecai Feinermann, he tried to wangle something out of Leyb Abrahamovich, he talked it over with Moyshe Kahan, and he even lowered himself so far as to ask Baynish Zisovich.

'Solomon Fuchs?' said Moyshe Kahan as they stood in front of the *mikvah*.* 'He's just laughing at you.'

'Laughing at me? Why?'

'Because you don't know what to do.'

'What's he going to do himself?'

'You don't think he'd tell me that, do you?'

Father went off to Mukachevo, he went as far as Berehovo and Chust, but he was no wiser when he returned. Everywhere he went he faced the same panic-stricken reaction and gesticulations, the same gaze fixed on the middle distance, the same shrugging of the shoulders.

'What do the Fuchses say about it?'

'What do the Fuchses say about it?' Leyb Abrahamovich replied. 'How should I know? What are the Fuchses likely to say about it? Solomon says the rest can do as they like but he isn't going to change his money.' 'The rest' could mean nobody else but Joseph Shafar. 'He says he knows what he's doing. And he's making fun of you.'

Father walked back and forth in Grandfather's room. 'What am I to do, Father? There's nothing left to buy and money's still worth something.'

Grandfather's white hand lying on the bedcover turned over and back: palm upwards, back upwards. 'If you've no faith in your own luck, change half and risk the rest.'

'No!' Mother wept out loud in bed at night.

The Jews arranged a strictly confidential meeting in Svalava, at the home of Ephraim Weiss. A secret invitation was sent to Budapest, to Dr Mór Rosenfeld, the financial expert, and those in the know were nervously arguing whether he would be able to cross the frontier or not. But he came in the end.

About forty men, influential Jews from far and wide, gathered that evening in two of Weiss's rooms, behind drawn blinds, shuttered windows and heavy curtains.

Joseph Shafar and Solomon Fuchs were there from Polana, and the Svalava rabbi came in his silk gown. They smoked heavily in their agitation and the room was soon filled with smoke.

Ephraim Weiss brought in the guest, a prosperous-looking man in spectacles, of citified appearance, without sidecurls and without a hat. Suddenly aware of this lack, Ephraim Weiss ran into the hall and came back with a hat, placing it on the visitor's head with a reassuring smile. The stranger laughed and pressed the hat down on his head; he nodded his thanks to his host and the others smiled too. He began to make their acquaintance, and each of them tried to buttonhole him for as long as possible. In all eyes there was the same question: what am I to do? Finally the Svalava rabbi got him to himself.

In a little while Mór Rosenfeld excused himself and left the rabbi; he sat down at the table. The tension in the room was so great that the sudden silence seemed about to crack. Taking a pile of cuttings pasted on sheets of paper from his despatch case he placed them by his right hand. Then he began to speak.

First he felt bound to stress that he had no connection with the Hungarian government, nor was what he was going to say official propaganda. He was a Jew and knew only too well that for the Jews there was little to choose between one European state and another; from the national and religious point of view it did not matter to them where they lived. Nevertheless, he had been invited and would be pleased to tell his fellow Jews all he knew. He was an honest man and he knew that very serious conclusions might be drawn from his words, and therefore, at the very outset, he wished to emphasise one more point: he thought that, as a bank manager, he was perhaps better and more reliably informed than other people. Nevertheless he could not bear any responsibility, since these were mainly matters of secret diplomacy and not even *his* information was first-hand. In any case, his distinguished listeners themselves would have to determine the degree of significance to be attributed to the documents he wished to read. He also wished to point out that among his audience there were wise men with information from other sources, and that it would be to their mutual benefit if in the course of discussion facts could be compared with facts, and views put forward for both sides of the argument.

Having hedged himself about with provisos, he was ready to begin. He talked of the international situation, of fresh alliances being made and new groups forming in Europe, of the position of Czechoslovakia, of the hopes of Hungary to regain the territory taken from her, or at least part of it, of the position of Sub-Carpathian Ukraine, still vague and unclarified. He backed it all up with numerous quotations, citing speeches made by the prime ministers and foreign ministers of England, France, Italy, Germany and Poland, and quoting English, American and Italian papers – the pile of newspaper cuttings at his right hand gradually moved over to his left. Speaking of the general view in Hungary, he said there was only one thing he could say with assurance: that if the Hungarians came back here their political leaders were determined not to accept Czechoslovak currency for exchange, and to declare a traitor to the nation anyone who had changed his money, and deal with him accordingly.

He talked for two hours and a quarter. The air in both rooms was so full of smoke that people could not breathe, and whenever the door was opened smoke poured into the hall as though damp straw was smouldering. Heads perspired under velvet and felt hats. No, he would not say whether the Hungarians would return or not. He only said, *if* they come back. He would not say whether they should change their money or not. But it was clear enough.

'The white!' Something seemed to shout in Joseph Shafar's mind: 'Don't change!'

The speaker invited his hearers to discuss the matter openly but nobody dared to speak. He waited for a while, a considerate smile on his lips as he ran his eyes over the assembled faces and then stretched his hand out towards them in kind impatience, palm upwards: W-e-e-ell?

'We are not changing, in Berehovo,' Gutman Davidovich of Berehovo said nonchalantly to those near him.

'I made up my mind not to change long ago!' Solomon Fuchs of Polana declared energetically.

Joseph Shafar's heart thumped.

The Czechophiles, who were known to be changing their money, the very men who, in the words of the speaker, should have had knowledge of the other point of view, said nothing.

'Why don't you say anything?' Jacob Rappaport of Torun shouted at them; he was small and thin, with a greying russet beard, and when he shouted he sounded as though he was about to cry. He called across to Mendl Leybovich of Soymo: 'Why are you holding your tongue now? When we're alone you make my head whirl with your noise!' Rappaport of Torun had recently been paid 460,000 crowns for timber he had floated down the Rika to Chust.

Leybovich of Soymo simply shrugged his shoulders and kept his thoughts to himself: he was no good at public speaking, was he? He hadn't got a bag full of press-cuttings, had he? It was all a matter of inspiration.

The meeting lasted until long after midnight. By then the air was almost too thick to breathe. Men were debating excitedly in pairs and shouting from group to group. For the sake of his eyes the Svalava rabbi had already left, and the guest from Budapest, the centre of interest, looked as though he was longing for his bed, too.

Little Jacob Rappaport of Torun had seized him firmly by the coat-button, and there were tears in his voice as he asked: 'Shall I change or not?'

Mór Rosenfeld smiled and shrugged his shoulders imperceptibly. He tried to explain something but Jacob Rappaport refused to listen. 'No, no! . . . Shall I change or not?'

Don't change! Joseph Shafar felt like shouting at him out loud.

The timber merchant just could not get a direct answer out of the city man. Jacob Rappaport scuttled through both the rooms, weaving his way in and out between the groups of men and those standing alone, and came back again to Mór Rosenfeld: 'Shall I change or not?' Eventually he broke down in a fit of hysterical weeping.

They kept it up until morning. Even then they could not break the party up, and after Ephraim Weiss had taken his guest to his room the others continued the debate on the street in the light of dawn. Father, tired and sleepy, arrived back in Polana with Yankel towards evening of the following day. Mother ran down the balcony to meet him.

'I'm not going to change, Mother,' said Joseph Shafar as he jumped down from the trap.

'The Lord's name be praised!'

The deadline drew near. The Hungarians had still not returned, and every day it was Czech policemen or excise men, in their flat caps with rifles over their shoulders, who patrolled the road outside the Shafars' house in pairs. Father had made his mind up now. The final date came and went. The Shafars did not change.

The Czechs issued a new notice: now they were offering to exchange at the rate of 100:50 – fifty Czechoslovak crowns to one hundred Hungarian.

'Change all you've got,' Grandfather said from his bed. 'The Czechs are putting their terms up; they feel sure of themselves. Do it quickly!'

'I won't.'

The news from Hungary was reassuring: don't be in too much of a hurry. Wait and see! Only a couple of weeks, now. The revision of the peace treaties would only be a matter of weeks.

Then the Czechs offered 100:25. Then 100:10.

'It's still not too late to change,' whispered Grandfather in a weak voice.

Then nobody would touch Hungarian money at all. That was really the end. Father did not have the lucky touch.

Solomon Fuchs had changed all his money. At 100:100. He even changed at 100:25 the small reserve he had cautiously kept back in case the Hungarians came after all, so as not to be without any Hungarian money at all.

'What have Abraham and Joseph Shafar got to say about it?' he asked Kahan the *beder* as they stood in front of the *mikvah*, and was careful not to show his amusement. He knew he could rely on Moyshe to pass it on to Joseph.

Father had two hundred and five thousand at home in cash. It was Hanele's dowry. He still has it. It is stuffed into a paper sack large enough to hold ten kilograms of goods, tucked away behind the dishes in the bottom of the dresser in the best room. When gentlemen come down from the city on official business, and for some strange reason do not get out at the Fuchses' but go on until they reach the Shafars' place, and if there is someone among them who knows the story of this money and asks Father to show them the stuff, Father fetches the big paper sack, designed to hold ten kilograms of goods, and the gentlemen gleefully dig their hands into the banknotes of thousand-, hundred-, and fifty-crown denominations, Hanele's dowry. They laugh and Father smiles sadly out of politeness.

If you see nothing around you, day in, day out, but the kitchen and rooms with the beds turned down ready, nothing but the farmyard criss-crossed with the tracks of the fowls, with the cows driven out in the morning and coming back of their own accord in the evening, with the horses that need the gate opening for them; if you see through the window nothing but the orchard where washing hangs out to dry on lines stretched between deformed apple trees; and if, when you want to get a better view, your eyes meet only the high mountains lining the valley on both sides, then you are surprised how short a time there is between '*Gute woch*' and '*Gut shabos*',* between one visit to the *mikvah* and the next, between *Yom Kippur* and *Rosh-ha-shanah.**

The years flew by. Grandfather had been dead a long time. Father had sold two of the mills and some of the farm land, and had married Etelka off to a suitor from Košice, with a flourish.

Soon afterwards he lost two of the cases he was fighting against Fuchs, and not long after that he lost the third. The costs were tremendously high; Mother went about wringing her hands and Father had to sell the third mill and more land.

Then, when Hanele was getting to be a big girl, he married Bálinka off to a suitor from Mukachevo. The other father-in-law was a hard man, and his son behaved disgracefully, too. Even though he and Bálinka got on well and have fine children, Mother has still not forgiven him. They insisted on the dowry, twice they threatened to break off the engagement, and in the end Father gave them what they asked. He had to sell more

39

land, and because he wanted to keep at least some of it, got himself into debt. Perhaps it was partly to spite the Fuchs family, for nobody wanted to marry their short fat daughters. In vain did the *shadkhan*, the match-maker, bring suitors to view Sura, who would soon be an old maid; it was indeed the only pride of Hanele's parents, now, that they could find good husbands for their beautiful daughters.

But then – then came the greatest catastrophe of all. Father lost the biggest, last and most costly of all his cases against Fuchs. Grandfather's times were long gone, and now the wealthy Solomon Fuchs could afford more witnesses. That defeat turned Father into a beggar.

When the decision of the highest court of appeal was delivered in writing to both parties, all five Fuchs girls, short and fat, put on their best clothes: twenty-three-year-old Cissie and twenty-one-year-old Laja wore white cambric, Cissie with a cherry-coloured sash and Laja with a green one; Sura, the eldest, put on her astrakhan coat open all down the front, although it was July. They powdered their faces and reddened their lips to a Cupid's bow, put on all the jewels they and their mother possessed, rings, bracelets, brooches – under her fur coat Sura's gold chain could be seen dangling right to her waist – and set out to parade up and down in front of the Shafars' house. Four hundred paces there and four hundred paces back, along the deserted weekday Polana street; they talked and laughed merrily and never so much as glanced at the Shafar house. Only their brother Benjie always dropped back two paces when they reached the shop, stood still facing the Shafar's house, and gave a piercing whistle with his fingers in his mouth. They walked back and forth slowly four or five times and sailed off home again, leaving Benjie to stand with his feet astride in front of the shop, trying to whistle a complete song on two fingers.

Mother, an old woman now, as thin as a shadow in the last few years, was in the kitchen picking things up and putting them down again unthinkingly. In the room beyond, Hanele was crying by the window. She could see Father outside, running hither and thither in the orchard, and the green of the leaves seemed to make his face even greyer.

From then on things went from bad to worse, swiftly and without respite.

Solomon Fuchs enjoyed the confidence of the new authorities, co-operated with them and was going to run the election campaign. He was given a licence to sell tobacco as well as all other licences issued to the village. He built himself a house in which there was a new shop and a real inn, not just a bar; here the policemen and excise men would sit, with the timber overseers and any gentlemen who happened to come from the town. The Ruthenians had set up their own co-operative shop and bar: Our Own Shop. Nobody came to the Shafars' any more, not even those whose credit was bad with the Fuchses and in the co-op, for they knew Father could not give them anything on credit at all. Most of the drawers and shelves in the shop were empty now. There was one single sack of cattle salt standing there, one dusty box of the cheapest sweets, an untidy heap of rusty chains in one corner. On the wall hung a bucket that also

41

served in the house, and on the shelves – which held only a couple of bolts of cloth and half a dozen red handkerchiefs – a notice had been nailed: 'The property of the firm of Herschkovich and Löbl, Mukachevo.' You could have bought the whole lot for twenty crowns. When wealth went, honour went with it, and now, if the rabbi comes to the village, the kind and friendly rabbi, who used to stroke Hanele's hair, he too stops at the Fuchses'.

To save her parents from poverty, Hanele's sister in Košice had the heavily mortgaged house and the last bit of land transferred to her name, while the cow in the byre (the only one left), the poultry in the farmyard and the two silver Sabbath candlesticks had become, formally at least, the property of her sister in Mukachevo. That, at least, was a safeguard against the bailiffs' demands. Father was now nothing more than a poor labourer living in a great big dilapidated house.

Hanele was maid-of-all-work, cook, seamstress, laundress; she got up at half-past three to drive the cow and the geese to pasture, and she didn't go to bed until eight at night after she had seen to the milking.

It is the purpose in life of a Jewish woman to bear sons, one of whom may be the Messiah. Hanele's mother had not fulfilled this mission. Would Hanele fulfil it? Those frights, the Fuchs girls, unlovely, ill-made and ill-favoured, with hairy nostrils, eyes sunk in fat, and perspiring hands – if those bad-tempered shrews with their ugly noses could not find suitors worthy of their aristocratic hands (and they wouldn't! they wouldn't! they wouldn't!) when they were past thirty,

they would at least be able to set some poor fellow on
his feet with Solomon's money. But who would marry
Hanele? When thoughts like that jerk you into wakeful-
ness in the night, and you suddenly hear the clappers of
Grandfather's mills, you feel like burying your head in
the pillows and weeping with sorrow and anger. Yes,
indeed: who would marry an inn where no one comes
to drink, a shop where no one comes to buy, a house that
belongs to an unknown brother-in-law? Could she
marry any of the local boys, who were nothing and
would never be anything and never know where the next
day's meals were coming from? Or would a miracle
happen? Hanele wept, but she was only seventeen, and
she still believed in miracles.

On the Sabbath afternoon, as long as the weather was
not too bad, the Jewish girls of Polana would put on the
finest things they had and the boys would put on decent
clothes, and they would promenade up and down the
valley road, the quarter of a mile or so to the forester's
cottage and back. The girls stayed in groups and so did
the boys, smiling at each other and flirting mildly when
they met. It was the only form of amusement Polana had
to offer. Shloym Katz was flirting with Hanele. She
thought he was attractive. He had fine teeth, a cheerful
smile, and nice clothes.

One evening, when the cow had come back from
pasture (Bryndusha was clever enough to find her own
way and tinkle the bell round her neck for them to come
and open the gate) and Hanele had followed the cow
into the stall to milk it, Shloym came to see her. She

turned on her milking stool where she sat by the cow's udder. He was smiling in the doorway.

'Get out of here! You're in my light,' she said sharply.

He went inside. He told her funny stories and laughed, and she laughed with him, and it was all very friendly. In the half-light Bryndusha smelt soft and warm and the milk spurted into the foaming pail. All at once Shloym bent over and gave Hanele a kiss. She blushed to the roots of her hair. 'You just wait till I tell Mother!'

For the next few days he would wait for her in the chilly early morning, before it was even quite light, when she turned the cow and the geese out to pasture. And he started coming into the shop for little things.

Hanele said nothing to Mother at all, but Mother sensed something was in the air. She took over the cow in the morning and saw to the milking, too; it was she who sold Shloym his matches or his piece of soap, and on the Sabbath she accompanied Hanele on her walks. Shloym? Shloym Katz, who could only wear nice clothes because his lame father spent the summer in Prague, Brno and Bratislava, with the rabbi's recommendation, begging? Shame!

One day Hanele's sister invited her to Košice, for the wedding of one of her husband's relatives. Etelka took on a home dressmaker, they looked through all the fashion magazines, and then they made Hanele a frock: a lovely full frock of voile. Everyone admired Hanele at the wedding. She had plenty of dancing partners and the young men all told her she had beautiful eyes. But that was all. Etelka's husband was worried about the house in Polana and was always complaining to his café cronies; everybody knew who Shafar of Polana was. A fortnight later Hanele returned home . . . What's to be done with her, Mother?

There are four who are dead while still alive: the poor, the blind, the leper, and the one who is childless. It looked as though Hanele would be doubly dead.

Is there anything worse than to betray the God of Israel and go over to another religion?

There is.

Surely you know the instructive story from the Talmud that Pinches Yakubovich is always telling? About the rabbi at the crossroads?

A wise rabbi was walking along a road. A *goy* overtook him in a cart, and offered to give him a lift. They drove on together in friendly fashion until they came to a crossroads. There was something hanging there, well, you know the sort of thing, the man hanging from a piece of wood, it's to be found at most crossroads. The *goy* did not lift his hat. 'Why did you not uncover your head?' asked the rabbi after a while. 'Why should I uncover my head?' the man laughed. 'I don't believe in anything.' 'Stop the cart, if you please, then,' said the rabbi, 'and I will get out. I could ride with a man who professes a different religion from my own, but I am afraid to travel with a man who professes no faith, for such a man is capable of anything.'

Alas! Times were such in Polana nowadays that nobody cared to listen to the wonderful tales Pinches Yakubovich had to tell. Irreligion had found its way into Polana . . .

Where did it come from, in God's name? It is hard to say. We only know its last resting-place before it finally found the way to Polana. That was in Mukachevo, in the irreligious Hebrew high school there. Irreligion in the form of Zionism.

It always takes a long time before the waves which bear human thought, whether sight or sound waves, electric, radio or some as yet unknown to us, get as far as this gulley in the mountains covered with virgin forest, this gulley where someone once had the idea of planting Polana. A hundred times, even a thousand times on their way they are thrown back by the wrong slope of the Carpathians; they flow back to surge forward again, and in the end they always find some valley through which to pass. What does time matter, though, in the valley of exile where all are awaiting the Messiah? And where the only thing that happens is the passage of days and months?

The promised land of their fathers, remembered in daily ritual for two thousand years, in hundreds of gestures and thousands of words of prayer, recalled every Sabbath by sniffing its scent from a stoppered flask, lured them. And so did the thought of the grapes of the land of Canaan, each cluster so heavy that they had to bear it on a staff between two of them.

'Oh unhappy nation of Israel!' cried the rabbis. 'Has error found its way into your midst again? Have you forgotten the vow the Lord demanded of you when He sent you into exile? That you should never try to get back to the promised land, but wait for the Lord to send you the Messiah who would lead you back? The men who would lead you to Palestine now are making the chosen people a nation like any other, calling down the wrath of the Lord and rousing the nations to new wrath against us.

'Unhappy people of Israel! Once more a new idol has been put up in your midst, another golden calf: false knowledge. You can declare the earth is round and that it turns on its axis; you can believe that man is descended from the animals and the world is older than our calendar. Fools! Keep your figures to yourselves, we are not interested in them, and we are not going to discuss your proofs. For we know that your knowledge differs from one century to another, and what was true for you yesterday is no longer true today, what is true today will not be true tomorrow. We know that the nations of the unbelievers, who have no other way to knowledge, use these ways to find out what we received in revelation thousands of years ago, and that all their knowledge, if it is true, cannot achieve anything after all its wanderings and errors and new wanderings but what we have long known without their learned men: God! God! God! Blessed be His name!

'You proclaim that the nation must be preserved, yet you cut off your sidecurls, you shave, you eat unclean food and say Saturday is no different from any other day. Fools! Have you forgotten that the Lord scattered like the sands of the desert nations far greater than the nation of Israel, and wiped them from the face of the earth (where are the Babylonians, where are the Romans?), while we are still living because we have kept

47

the commandments which the Lord our God gave us to keep us from being as others are?

'Get from our midst! May a curse fall upon you! May your wells dry up and your women be barren!'

Nothing like that had even occurred to the people of Polana. The whole thing began in a light-hearted way, more as a joke than anything else.

It happened that the brother of the cobbler, Leyb Abrahamovich, away in Cherenin somewhere, fell ill – the same Leyb Abrahamovich who used to sing in such a hearty voice on the Sabbath evening: 'Rititi! Tarara! Come, my friend, to meet the Bride!' Leyb Abrahamovich's brother was also a cobbler. When he was taken to hospital in July, Leyb took over his work for a time; Polana could wait, and he couldn't leave his brother's family in trouble. *Gemilut khasadim.*

In Cherenin there lived a wealthy merchant and inn-keeper, Selig Wolf, who had twelve children; with himself, his wife and his sisters that made sixteen people, and they all wore shoes. That's something to thank the Lord for, a customer like that! Selig Wolf took on Leyb Abrahamovich to repair the family's shoes and make new ones ready for the autumn. He cleared a shed in the yard and gave the cobbler leather, bristles and pegs from the shop. In one corner he piled up all the old shoes, Leyb brought his brother's tools along, and sat down to his cobbling. Selig Wolf had a son, Hersch, who was in the fifth form of the Mukachevo High School. He spent whole mornings sitting on the threshold of the shed, talking to Leyb Abrahamovich. Perhaps his father had told him to keep an eye on the cobbler, perhaps he was bored during the holidays, or perhaps he just wanted to show off his knowledge. He told Abrahamovich about the world, about science and Zionism and socialism; he read newspapers aloud to him and showed him pictures in books. Of course, if a *goy* had told him all those things – well, they believe all kinds of nonsense – but this was a Jew, a student from Mukachevo who was going to be a doctor one day! Leyb Abrahamovich, hungry for knowledge, learned of horizons he had never dreamed of, and launched himself towards them with stubborn fury, like a buccaneer. There was a lot of debate and little work going on in the shed. 'All right, all right! Wear yourself out for a capitalist!' Hersch would say. And so he completely turned the cobbler's head.

In this state of muddle-headedness Leyb returned to Polana that autumn, when his brother was sent home from hospital. There he started talking all kinds of nonsense, saying that the earth was round and that it revolved on its axis. Leyb Abrahamovich was dreadfully hairy; his broad gingery beard seemed to start right up by his eyes, he had enough hair on his head for three men, and when he stood there in the street in front of his cottage, explaining this new scientific theory to the Jews standing around and laughing, his hair seemed to stand out all over his great leonine face, and his eyes blazed. When his audience laughed even louder ('Why, you half-wit, the houses would fall down!'), he dashed angrily into the cottage and returned with a cloth and a mug of water. Taking the corners of the cloth between his fingers he put the mug in the fold and then started swinging it wildly through the air, to prove that the houses would not fall down. The Jews nearly burst their sides with laughing.

Old Mordecai Yid Feinermann did not regard these wild ideas with amusement. One evening, in the half-light of the synagogue on a weekday, after the evening *ma'ariv** prayer had been said, he motioned Leyb into a corner. Jabbing at his chest with his long forefinger the old man said slowly and sternly: 'You are going about the village talking nonsense. People are laughing at you. I do not laugh. This is the way dissension in Jewry always starts. I warn you. If you do not stop, the community will have to take steps and the rabbi will certainly take steps. Do not forget that!'

He turned away, dignified and saintly, and moved back into the half-light of the synagogue.

However, Leyb Abrahamovich was ready to lay down his life for the new truth that had been revealed to him. God knows why it should be cobblers, of all people, who get inflamed by revolutionary ideas; nobody has studied this fact yet, but perhaps it has something to do with their craft, with the smell of leather, and with their courage and manliness. Leyb Abrahamovich went back to Cherenin for fresh wisdom. As soon as the Sabbath ended, before dawn every Sunday morning, he marched off down the valley road, thirty kilometres there and thirty kilometres back; it was late at night before he got home – and all so he could talk to Hersch and get off his mind the troublesome ideas that had been bothering him all week: 'What sort of light did God create the first day, if it wasn't till the fifth day that He made the sun and the moon?' or 'If you were to dig an enormous hole in the earth and if you were to drop a cobbler's hammer into that hole, would it come out on the other side or would it stop halfway and stay hanging in the middle of the air there?' Some of Leyb's questions went right to the very foundations of philosophy, and not even the all-knowing Hersch could answer them: 'You said there was nothing outside the universe. What do you mean by nothing? Is there darkness out there? Darkness is something, isn't it?' All their discussions somehow ended up in politics, and that was what Abrahamovich was full of when he got home every Sunday night. All kinds of people began gathering in his cobbler's shop to talk things over: Srul Nakhamkes the smith, young Eizigovich, Moshko Mendlovich, the elegant Shloym Katz. Leyb Abrahamovich explained everything. He started talking about the rich and the poor, about why the Fuchses should have everything and the rest of them nothing, about Zionism, about the colonisation of Palestine, about brotherhood and a new life.

'Is it really true that the world is round?'
'There's proof of it!'
'A *goy*'s proof.'
'Jewish proof, too.'

Leyb Abrahamovich! A mad cobbler, a man without learning, whom nobody respected, whom nobody even bothered about before all this began! What had happened to the shoemaker, that all at once he ceased to fear the wisdom of Mordecai Yid Feinermann, the holiness of Pinches Yakubovich, or the might of Solomon

Fuchs? Was the community to be rent in twain because of Leyb Abrahamovich?

It was.

One Sunday in Cherenin, Hersch Wolf was suddenly struck by an idea; he laughed out loud and clapped his hands together. 'Wait a minute! I'll get Father's trap out before the end of the holidays and drive round to pick up a couple of the lads. We'll set up a Zionist meeting in your mouldy little village. We'll make Polana sit up! Abrahamovich, it'll be worth seeing the fun!'

One day they really did drive up, six of them, with Hersch Wolf; they were *halutz** youth, Socialist Zionists. They opened the meeting in the afternoon, near the *mikvah*, where the brook flows into the stream and where there is a flat stretch of stones and pebbles on the point between them, washed up by the spring floods.

Almost the whole of the Jewish community of Polana was there. Craftsmen, labourers, carters, lumberjacks, farmers, shopkeepers and beggars (and often all these trades rolled into one), with sidecurls and without, in gowns and in ordinary clothes or just in the rags that remained, the members of the forty-eight families with a *tallith* in the synagogue, not counting the few widows' families. They came with their wives and children. They crowded the pebbly meeting-place, they stood on the footbridge over the brook, and they hung about on the road. Mischievous children were making a noise and Riva Kahan and Benjie Fuchs were trying to push each other into the water, egged on loudly by the onlookers.

Mordecai Yid Feinermann was not there, nor was Pinches Yakubovich. Neither Joseph Shafar nor Solomon Fuchs came. The Fuchs girls were there, though, parading up and down the road, Sura with her usual sour-sweet smile. Hanele was with Rifka Eizigovich and Miriam Herschkovich, and Shloym and the students flocked round them; there was a great deal of joking and Hanele was glad of the chance to laugh freely just when the Fuchs girls were about.

'Well, what about it, young lady with the beautiful eyes?' one of the students said. 'Are you coming with us to Palestine?'

'Do you think I wouldn't?' Hanele replied. 'I'd set off this minute!'

'Would you really go?' asked Shloym Katz, and gazed into Hanele's face longer than was modest.

Then young Eizigovich dragged a table up and the oldest of the students swung himself up on it in athletic fashion; people hurried down from the road, and the meeting began.

The student made a speech. He began with a smile, in a friendly manner, to gain his listeners' sympathy; this he succeeded in doing, with all who were not prejudiced beforehand. They listened to him with close attention. Even the mischievous boys were quiet and listened to what he had to say, even Benjie and Riva – Riva was now soaking wet, Benjie having finally won and pushed him into the water. The speaker described the unity of the whole of Jewry. The sufferings and persecution of the Jews in *galuth*.* In colourful phrases he described the poverty of these very parts, the unemployment, the destitution, the hunger, the high mortality rate among children and grown-ups. His listeners were moved, feeling that he was speaking of each of them, individually. These men and women, who had never heard an orator before except for wandering preachers and students of the rabbinical schools, were roused by his eloquence, and a mother who had taken to heart the remark about infant mortality began to weep. Do we all suffer to the same degree? The speaker raised his voice. No! he thundered his own reply. Like all other nations, the Jewish nation is divided: into the rich and the poor. The poor Jews suffer twice over: for their Jewish faith and for their poverty. The rich are well off even in *galuth*; they do not want to see anything changed and they need to seek no way out. Their role in life is the same as that of the rich everywhere: the exploitation of the poor, exploitation of their work, grinding them down by raising prices . . .

Two paces beyond the edge of the crowd of listeners stood the daughters of Solomon Fuchs. Baynish Zisovich went and stood next to Sura. Perhaps because he was a relation of the Fuchs family, even if only a very distant one, or perhaps because he owed them money, Baynish took up a reactionary attitude at this meeting, as one who had decided his views beforehand.

'Baynish, ask him whether the earth really turns,' said Sura.

Baynish hastened to shout: 'Hey, you there, Moshko or whatever they call you – is it true that the earth turns round?'

Some of those present, remembering Abrahamovich's tricks with the cloth and the mug of water, began to laugh, but most of them disliked the interruption.

Leyb Abrahamovich's whiskers stood on end, his eyes flashed, and he started up from the table The students held him back.

The speaker drew himself up, pointed a finger at Baynish, and called out in a theatrical voice: 'Yet it does move!'

He burst into laughter himself at his plagiarism, the students were laughing at the joke, and in a moment everybody down there by the brook was laughing.

To be able to get to the reason for his being there at all, the speaker had to go back to where he had been interrupted: to the rich, who do not want any change and do not need to seek any way out. 'But there is a way out for the poor and downtrodden!' he cried, and fell silent to give his hearers a chance to prepare themselves for what was to come. 'Yes, there is a way out: Zionism!' He talked about Palestine, about the new homeland, about equality in life and work, about a land where, even if it were not rich, there was enough work for all and prosperity for everyone, about the land of freedom! He spoke with enthusiasm, his eyes flashing and his gestures passionate, working up both himself and his audience.

'I say, Baynish,' said Sura softly, 'when we've gone, ask him if he eats pork.' The Fuchs girls moved away with mincing steps. They climbed back on to the path and set off for home. In a little while they slowed down, so as not to miss anything.

'Do you eat the flesh of pigs?' Baynish shouted.

That really made the people angry. They started shouting. Leyb Abrahamovich struggled with the students who were trying to hold him back, freeing his hands and kicking them on the knee and shouting in a terrible voice: 'I'll throw him in the brook, him and those little bitches of his.'

For Leyb Abrahamovich was a hero, a true hero. For the sake of the truth he found he was ready to sacrifice not only his life, but even Solomon Fuchs – his best customer.

At this time of the year the shadow of the mountains falls across the valley very early. When all the speakers had had their say and the meeting was over, the Jews of Polana went their ways in deep twilight. They were silent, overcome by all the new ideas and weighing up the pros and cons in their minds.

Mother had come to the meeting three times, her eyes searching among the crowd, but she had not been able to wait till the end, and now she had missed her chance. Hanele was on her way home in the middle of the group of students. Shloym Katz was at her side, trying to touch her hand as they walked along.

'Hanele, why can I never talk to you?' he asked sadly.

'You know how it is, Shloym. Mother never lets me go anywhere.'

They dropped behind a little.

'Hanele, I'm so fond of you,' he took her hand in the gathering darkness. 'I don't think of anything else. I don't dream of anything else. I can't live without you.'

'I like you, too, Shloym, you know I do,' she answered, and dropped her eyes. 'I've liked you for a long time, now. I dream about you, too, and I think about you. A lot, Shloym, I really do. But what good is it?'

'Hanele!' he squeezed her hand.

'Can you come and ask Father for my hand?'

'Of course I can,' he said resolutely.

'Who would keep us?' she said sadly. And in her heart of hearts she added, will your Father go begging for us, too, when there are six more of you at home?

They walked along in silence, holding hands in the darkness and swinging their arms. It was actually Hanele who made the first movement, and the hands swinging up and down gave force to her question and its answer.

It was a little while before Shloym said tentatively and hopelessly: 'Would you go to Palestine with me, though, Hanele?'

Oh, the nonsense people talk, she thought, but aloud she said: 'I don't know. I might.'

They were drawing near the Shafar house.

'Come on,' said Hanele, and pulled her hand free. 'Mother will be coming out.'

'No . . .' Shloym called after her beseechingly.

She took a few quick steps and caught up with the students and her friends and mingled with them. Mother was there now, her eyes searching the darkness to see who her daughter was walking with. Hanele said goodnight to them all, but somehow forgot to give Shloym her hand. The students kept the prettiest girl in the village company all the way home, and as the door closed behind her they called out '*Shalom!*' in loud voices. Mother was smiling happily. Was anybody calling '*Shalom!*' after the Fuchs girls?

Father asked what the meeting had been like.

'They're right,' declared Hanele, and shook her curls.

But her father shook his head: 'No, they are not. The earth does not turn. Leyb Abrahamovich is mad.'

Perhaps he was, but his influence grew day by day. He carried his head high now, his gait had changed, and there was a proud gleam in his eye. Now his thin wife, humble and sparing of words, would sometimes start talking to the neighbours on the street, and even laughing, so that Sura Fuchs in the shop shook her head nastily and said: 'Well, just look at our cobbler's lady!' Of course, it was enough to make you weep to see the state of the floor in the Abrahamovich's room, and all the smoke in the evening, making the children cough as they slept up there on top of the stove, but was it not a wonderful feeling to be the wife of the leader who would one day enter Palestine at the head of the community of Polana? For now her husband had set up an organisation and there were regular meetings held in their cottage.

Leyb made speeches: Palestine! The land of our fathers! Freedom! Prosperity! Happiness! Away from poverty, away from the exploiters, away from the darkness of *galuth*! If the Messiah comes soon, we shall be there in the promised land to welcome him!

Half the village had been affected by the new teachings, even if not totally convinced. For once a man begins to say 'There's something in that,' then things are getting serious. The Jews were even arguing at evening prayer in the synagogue.

One of the few people who realised that something unusual was taking place was Solomon Fuchs. He knew very well that public and private matters are closely bound up together, and that this was something that concerned not only Israel. It affected him personally as well.

He consulted the leaders of the community. Mordecai Yid Feinermann, that saintly old man, raised his forefinger, adopted a threatening expression, and said sternly: 'Something must be done about it!' But he did not know what. A plague on old Mordecai! He was hot enough on sidecurls, beard-cutting, candles, and harrying the *shohet** and the *beder!* When things started happening all he could do was to raise a finger! He consulted Pinches Yakubovich, too. Pinches, the cabbalist and follower of the rabbi of Belz, was full of melancholy and distress. 'You can do nothing with reason and proof,' he said in anguish. 'The only thing that will help is prayer. Pray! I, too, am praying.' Who was talking about reason and proof, you fool? said Solomon Fuchs to himself. So he was praying, was he? Ach! As though the Lord God could or even wanted to do everything himself.

Solomon Fuchs was neglecting his business. He left everything to his wife and daughters. Deep in thought he walked about the farmyard to the cattlesheds and back, mechanically opening the little gate to the vegetable garden and walking up and down there with his head hung low and his toes pointing inwards. He chewed on his tongue, scratching the back of his hand on the tip of his trimmed beard, stopping every now and again and twisting his hat round on his head bit by bit.

Cancel any work given to Abrahamovich and call in his debts, that was clear. Don't give the dissidents even a penn'orth of credit, call in their debts and don't give way until they declare publicly before the congregation in the synagogue that they are convinced the new teaching goes against God and against Israel, and until they forsake Abrahamovich. Of course! But what help would that be? His own interests were at stake now. Emigration was being preached. With every man leaving the country he lost a customer, that meant a couple of hundred a year, even with the poorest of them. There was even the danger of his losing customers without emigration. Abrahamovich had been seen buying at the Shafars' twice, Nakhamkes too, and young Katz was always in and out of the place. For the moment Shafar had got nothing to sell, thank God, and if a customer asked for a bit of soap he had to go into the kitchen and cut off a piece of his own. But yesterday the messenger who took letters across country to the post told him Shafar had written to his daughter in Mukachevo. He would not let Fuchs get hold of the letter, not even for two kilos of flour, not even for three. In fact, he said he wouldn't do it for a million, that sort of thing couldn't go on now, he was scared of the new Town Clerk. Anyway, what could Shafar be writing to his daughter about? Well, he could be writing to ask for a loan of a couple of hundred to stock the shop . . . Elections* were imminent. And he had asked for the monopoly of the sale of state maize!

The word 'elections' gave Fuchs an idea. He quickened his step as he trotted up and down between the rows of carrots, then he stopped. He twisted his hat around until it sat in its proper place again. That was it!

Next morning Solomon Fuchs drove into the town to see the District Commander.* When he found himself sitting opposite the Commander in his private office, on a well-padded chair (what must that have cost?), and explained what was going on in Polana, his host merely nodded.

'We know all about that. What do you suggest doing, Mr Fuchs?'

'Arrest Abrahamovich.'

'To the best of my knowledge there is no legal ground for arrest. The Social Democratic Party watches over the interests of the *halutz* Zionists. The students gave due notice of their intention to hold that meeting.'

'The elections are just round the corner, sir.'

'That is true. We are relying on you, of course. There are about a hundred and fifty Jewish voters in Polana. I trust you have no call to be dissatisfied with the authorities, Mr Fuchs. I will be open with you: our future favour depends on the way the elections turn out.'

Solomon Fuchs stood in the corridor of the District Commander's headquarters . . . Nothing doing . . . And he had applied for the monopoly in state maize sales! . . . He stood there twisting his hat round on his head. Nothing! He slapped his thigh.

Then he went to see the rabbi.

'Haven't you heard of the *mizrakhi** organisation?' asked the rabbi, turning his cup round in his hand, for he was just having tea. 'We have devoted a great deal of thought to the question of modern heresy, and we have come to the conclusion that Zionism can only be defeated by more Zionism. It would be too late now to fight against emigration, and so long as it is not confused with the question of the Messiah, we have no objections to it. Once Zionism is established, the only thing to do is to secure a leading role in it. So we have founded the *mizrakhi* organisation, which is also based on Zionism, but it is a strictly religious organisation. The leaders are young people from the best Jewish families. They have an attractive uniform, they cultivate sports and singing, and arrange social evenings. Your Sura had better establish a *mizrakhi* branch in Polana. Go and see Hidal Stein, he can tell you what to do. He'll send people to Polana to help, too.'

The rabbi had shown the way. And Hidal Stein gave him good advice.

Sura Fuchs set up a *mizrakhi* branch in Polana, comprising her sisters and her brother, Khaimek Zisovich and eight more young men and girls. Since in this case Solomon Fuchs was willing to give credit, they were able to make their uniforms, too: khaki hikers' shirts with a yellow Star of David on the sleeve.

A week later five young gentlemen in uniform arrived from the town. They arranged a picnic near the forester's cottage and there were speeches – though not as long as those of the students who had come to Polana – and songs were sung, and in the evening there was dancing to the gramophone at the Fuchses'. The young men gave bags of sweets to the young ladies, Sura's leadership smile was quite sweet and since during this political event she did not lose sight of the possibility of a secondary outcome to the visit from the town, in the evening she carefully made up her face and adorned herself with all her jewellery.

A week later Abrahamovich's *halutz* Zionists came to Polana again; not the students this time, they were all in Mukachevo, but men who knew that the tongue has other uses besides eating, and used it to good effect to castigate the *mizrakhi* traitors and the perfidious rich. Their main purpose, though, was to urge the people to organise. Organisation, organisation, organisation!

'What might that be?' Baynish Zisovich called out from a safe distance.

'Stupid, it means uniting, getting education, collecting money,' Shloym Katz answered for the speaker.

'So that's it!' Baynish burst out laughing.

He did not get away with it, though.

'How do you expect to get to Palestine without money, you fool?' Shloym Katz snapped at him.

They all laughed. Hanele most of all.

A few days later Abrahamovich and his closest disciples, Nakhamkes, Katz, Eizigovich and Mendlovich, received a lawyer's letter demanding payment of their debts to the firm of Solomon Fuchs, under threat of prosecution. Solomon Fuchs found it all the easier to take this step now that he no longer had to worry about losing their custom: all five had already defected to the Shafars'. It was true that for the five hundred crowns his Mukachevo son-in-law had sent him, accompanied by a nasty letter, Joseph Shafar could not stock his empty shop well, but at least it was enough for maize flour for everyday needs, and white flour for the Sabbath

63

barkhes,* and some salt. The lawyer's letters roused a lot of ill-feeling. Everyone knows what a job it is to pay a hundred and twenty, or even forty crowns, all at once, in cash, within a fortnight and what is more – shameless creatures! – five crowns to the lawyer for his services.

Public tension, reinforced by private anger, now began to manifest itself. One night, after two hours of deep sleep, Solomon Fuchs was awakened by the sound of a blow and the tinkle of broken glass.

'*Riboinoi shel oilom!** Lord of creation!' he shouted and jumped out of bed. The next moment he was lying on the floor with his hands covering his head.

Smash!

No, it was not a stone; a bottle had been flung and broken on the bars across the window.

His wife and the two daughters who slept with them let out yells of panic.

Smash! Smash! Smash! The panes cracked and glass flew all over the place. Then came two dull blows as stones rebounded from the iron bars.

Solomon Fuchs crawled on hands and knees to the wall by the windows, where he would be safe. 'Stop screaming!' he called to his wife and daughters. 'Get under the bedclothes and then slip carefully down to the floor and hide under the bed.'

The cries of his other daughters, and the weeping of the youngest, came from the next room. Stones rained noisily down on the floor.

The family eventually convened in the impenetrable darkness of the hall; some straightaway, some later. Here they were safe, for there were no windows and the doors were studded with iron. They were all trembling with cold and anxiety. Were they being attacked by one man or a thousand?

Now blows were heard from the other side of the building.

'The swine!' Sura was the first to speak. She was also the first to summon up courage to leave the hall and put some clothes on, and then to go and check whether the shutters of the shop were holding. Bending low, she crept through the rooms, cautiously peeping through the windows to see whether she could recognise anyone among the attackers. They had chosen a good night for the job, though; you could not see your hand before your face.

Smash! came again from the back of the house. Was there a single pane left whole?

They stayed up until morning, not daring to light the lamps or to go back to bed. They felt cold, and fumbled in the darkness for their blankets and eiderdowns, to wrap around themselves. There were glass, stones and broken bottles all over the floors.

They were not released until the first cart rattled over the cobbles and a Ruthenian peasant shouted in consternation through the bars of the smashed windows: 'Hey, you in there, what's happened?'

When they emerged they discovered that all their vegetables had been pulled up by the roots, scattered over the roadway and dirtied in the mud; when they went to look at the garden they found the beanstalks broken and the onion beds trampled to a juicy mess, as if a herd of cattle had been over it. To refresh their

65

throats, dry with anger, they drew water from the well, only to find it was undrinkable; someone had poured oil into the well.

Mrs Esther Fuchs said, with eyes flashing under her frowning brows, 'Who came to buy oil yesterday?'

'Yesterday, Mother?' Sura gave a grim smile. 'It could just as well have been a week ago.'

'On credit, too, most likely,' Cissie added spitefully.

The whole village soon knew what had happened, and little huddles of people formed in front of the Fuchs house; more and more came to join them. The police arrived, too, quick enough.

When the Shafars heard about it, Mother excitedly put on her best skirt and coat, and taking Hanele by the hand, said 'Come along!' They walked past the Fuchs house. The farm girls and the labourers were drawing water from the well with pails, and letting it run through the yard into the road. Solomon Fuchs stood in the doorway of the shop, between brightly coloured advertisements for soap and chicory.

Solomon Fuchs was not like Father, to be scared by two women, and dash off with his head between his hands to run up and down the garden. 'What have you got to stare at here?' he shouted to them.

'I was just thinking,' said Mother gently, and there was a break in her voice, 'that God always finds out the wicked.' She did not say whom she meant, however; it might have been the unknown culprit who had broken the windows that night.

Sura appeared at her father's side between the adverts. 'It's really only a trifle,' she smiled her sweet-sour smile. 'Or do you think we can't afford a few panes of glass, Mrs Shafar? God forbid it should come to that!'

And so a mad cobbler did indeed bring about schism in Israel. The whole village was torn apart and yet at the root of struggle there were but two just men.

Or was there only one? For saintly Mordecai Yid Feinermann, Polana's great hope in all evil times to come, had disappointed them. He neither saw nor heard. Is it not written in the Talmud that the lobes of the ear are soft only that they may be stuffed into the ears when evil things are spoken before us, and that the eyelids resemble curtains only that they may be dropped as a veil when unrighteous things are committed before our gaze? If we see nothing and hear nothing, then nothing happens. And for Mordecai Yid Feinermann nothing was happening. Or did he retire into his own heart because he knew that everything is foolish, vain and trifling that passes by without leaving trace or echo behind it, and that is not worthy to be admitted into the soul, which is immortal? When the bickering in the synagogue during the evening *ma'ariv* prayer grew too loud, he just prayed a little louder, and his head of old ivory and his yellowing beard swayed only a fraction faster.

Pinches Yakubovich, on the other hand, was a flame of passion and sorrow. A secret, unseen flame that nobody notices, but which burns, scorches and sears. That is the fate of a *lamet vav** (and was he one?). He knew that now was the time, or else the moment would pass for a long time to come. Never, since the beginning of the world, had such terrible things been seen, but if

God permits them, they can be but a forewarning of what is still to come. Israel had suffered much since the days of the destruction of the Temple. Yet those were sufferings of this world, drawing the chosen people even closer to their God, uniting them and making them even stronger to resist. What is bodily suffering and what are bodily things? Mist and smoke! Now the soul was at stake. What horrors had come upon Israel? Worshipping idols! False prophets! Schism! Brother's hand raised against brother! Whither do you hasten, oh unhappy people of Israel? To utter destruction and dispersal? Have you forgotten your God altogether?

Oh, try to understand what a burden it is when one man carries on his shoulders one thirty-sixth of the weight of the whole world. Try to understand what suffering it is for one man to nurture in his bosom one thirty-sixth of the sufferings of Israel! . . . Is he one of the thirty-six? . . . If he is, then the preservation or the destruction of the world rests with him, and were the whole world to go back he, of all people, must not move an inch from the place where God had placed him.

No, nobody wants to bother with Pinches and his parables and stories now. They have heard them all before, and shrug him off with a 'You and your fairytales!' Not even his old friend Moyshe Kahan – he has other worries now. Pinches Yakubovich no longer speaks in parables. He has said all there is to be said, and he knows that words cannot help now. Only prayer can help; prayer is mightier than the angels. And Pinches Yakubovich has given himself over to prayer.

In spite of Brana's shouts and curses – oh, Brana, Brana, who will be turned into a fish! – he has gone back to his habit of midnight prayer. There are thirty-six praying thus, in Melbourne, in New York, in Singapore and Peking, in Johannesburg, in the dead-end villages of Galicia or Siberia, all at the same moment lifting their voices in one united desperate prayer for the Messiah, in one urgent call which could not fail to penetrate the heavens. On Mondays and Thursdays, as *khtsot* was drawing near (that is the cabbalist way of referring to midnight), Pinches Yakubovich rises cautiously from his bed and puts on his shroud, the one which every Jew receives at the hands of his wife on his wedding day and which will go with him to the grave. He is getting ready to pronounce the terrible cabbalist prayer *Khurban bayit*, known only to the initiated, by which the Lord is to be pressed to send the Messiah. For on those days and at that moment, it is possible to win a great deal from the God-head. Pinches goes quietly into the hall, a chilly place with its floor of trodden clay, and lights candles in a circle around himself on the floor. Barefoot, in his long white shirt, he stands in the centre of the lights and begins to sway and sing in a tearful recitative the words: 'Woe to the children whose father has cursed them, and woe to the father whose children have deserted him.' Even these first words are nothing but blasphemy, a threat to the Lord. Pinches Yakubovich, bending backwards and forwards, laments the destruction of the Temple, lifts his hands to heaven, works himself up and reproaches God with all the sufferings of the Jewish exile; sweat pearls on his brow as he reminds the Lord of His promises, as he threatens Him, and falling to the ground he weeps and bangs his head on the clay floor, calling out: 'We have suffered long enough, we have fulfilled our mission, the hour has come, have mercy on us and send the Messiah!' At that same minute, that same moment, thirty-six chosen men unknown to each other and unknown by each other, at various places around the world are beating their heads upon the ground and wailing, lamenting and weeping, like Pinches Yakubovich: 'We have suffered long enough, we can go on no longer. Fulfil Thy promises! Send us the Messiah! Why art Thou slow? The Messiah! The Messiah!' And indeed, the scraggy, trembling body and the poor head with tear-stained eyes and red patches on the cheeks could hardly survive the horror of this moment, were not Pinches supported by the other thirty-five who have come together at the same moment. For it is one hour past midnight, and a Friday: in Shanghai as in Polana or Chicago, that much is certain.

'A plague on him! The lazy horse! The grave, that's all he's fit for! Fool! Fool!' Brana had come back from milking in the cowshed and was pulling the blankets off Pinches, throwing them on the floor and shouting and screaming: 'Up all night and snoring all day, not a hand's turn does he do the whole year round, leaving everything to me, all the work and drudgery he leaves to me, the horse-head! horse-head! horse-head! May the lightning strike you dead! May your teeth fall out, all except one and that one's going to hurt and hurt . . . fool, fool, fool!'

Oyoyoyoyoy!

Pinches Yakubovich humbly rises and humbly puts on his clothes.

Brana is screaming.

Humbly, without breakfast, Piches goes out. Scrawny, threadbare, looking like a fence-pole weather-beaten for years, with miserable sidecurls drooping in front of over-large ears, he goes to the Eizigoviches', the Katzes', the Zisoviches', sits a while and listens, says little and goes on his way again.

In Polana you have to look really ill for anyone to notice. Between the garden fences Pinches meets his friend Moyshe Kahan.

'Is anything wrong, Pinches?'

Can a *lamet vav* tell anyone his station? Can a *lamet vav* weep his sorrows out to anyone?

Pinches Yakubovich shakes his head.

'Brana's making life hard for you, I know what it's like', and under the impression that his own thoughts are not unlike those of Pinches, Moyshe scratches just behind a sidecurl. 'Well, what are you going to do about her?'

When Mother and Hanele came home that day and told him about the piles of broken glass in front of the Fuchses' house, about the trampled garden and the oil poured into the well, Father said: 'Perhaps they are right after all. You can join if you like.'

And so Hanele became a *halutz* Zionist.

There were about thirty members in the branch. From the Prague centre they were given pretty green money-boxes which they distributed round the houses and fixed to the wall; the keys were in the hands of the treasurer, Eizigovich. Collect money, Jews! Put your own farthings aside and beg from others! A little something every day. For every gift received, for every pleasure felt, for every bit of luck, for every kiss from your wife. We are building up our country, our life, our happiness!

When they met in Leyb Abrahamovich's cottage for their evening discussions he talked about equality and the brotherhood of the poor, and when he got excited he would fall into the *nigun** tone of prayer, dragging out the final syllables of his words.

Then Shloym Katz got up and read out loud the letter received from the Prague centre: the *mizrakhi* groups are traitors trying to sabotage the Zionist movement, and must be fought wherever they appear, in whatever circumstances and by whatever means; above all the young people must be taken care of, and when the right time comes an instructor will be sent to Polana to teach them *halutz* songs and round dances. The Polana branch must be the most militant in the whole of the Carpathians. In reply to the enquiry about keeping the Sabbath and about the food served in the communal canteens, the central office informed the branch that both the keeping of the Sabbath and the laws on the ritual purity of food were strictly observed in the *hakhsharas** of the Jewish farms in Slovakia and Ruthenia, but in the larger centres, in Prague and Brno, where the members of the group mostly worked in industry and where it was sometimes difficult to ensure ritual *kosher* food, these two customs were observed only as far as circumstances permitted; and why had Polana not yet sent in members' subscriptions?

The words about the Sabbath and the *kosher* food gave them a bit of a shock; in fact, quite a shock . . . Those were the two things the *mizrakhi* group were making most noise about. It looked as though they might even be right in some things . . .

Shloym Katz was the secretary of the branch. Mother came to fetch Hanele after the meetings. Hanele could never be sure Mother would not appear at any moment, but even so there was always the chance to slip out into the yard for a moment, to say a few words and steal a kiss.

Was it love? Hanele would ask herself in the night, when Grandfather's mills were singing in the silence. Love? She liked him as long as he was fun and made her laugh and – as long as he did not pester her. It is a nice feeling that there is someone who loves you, too. But she could not reconcile herself to the thought of that father-in-law. Lame in both legs, with a hump on his chest and his back, greedy and gluttonous, he had his beef and sausages sent from the town; he was the only one in the village to be fairly well off, except the Fuchs family. All through the summer he would stand at the entrance to the Prague market, propped on his crutches, bending to one side his Messiah-like head with its jet-black beard and great dark eyes, and gazing sorrowfully at the rich Jewesses coming out with shopping bags full. Hanele turned her nose up. Could you call that love?

'Are you going to Palestine, Hanele?' Shloym asked her in the darkness of the Abrahamovich's yard.

Hanele was leaning against a pile of timber prepared for winter fuel and looking up at the stars. 'I don't know, Shloym . . . I'd like to . . . People really live, in other places. I could see that when I stayed with my sister in Košice . . . This isn't life at all.'

'Will you go with me, Hanele?' he said ardently, and caught her hand.

This was a serious question, and Hanele could not fail to see what it meant. To ensure that the Palestine settlers multiplied, the Palestine Committee only accepted married men, and Shloym's words were an offer of marriage.

He had to wait a long time for his answer. Hanele leaned the soles of her feet against the pile of timber, too, and gazed at the stars right above her head. The meeting went on beyond the lighted windows. Shloym's heart was beating.

'With me! Come with me, Hanele!' he called ardently, and putting his arms around her pressed her to him and tried to kiss her. His kisses missed their mark, somewhere in the air.

'No! . . . No! . . . Let me go! . . . Let me go, Shloym!'

She managed to free herself. She went back inside, and with every nerve on edge, he followed her.

'Hanele . . .'

She stopped in the doorway and said calmly, although her voice trembled a little, 'You mustn't do that, Shloym, you know it's not right. I'd have to tell Mother.'

Then one day a letter came from the Prague centre, and caused great excitement among the *halutz* Zionists: a new *hakhshara* was being set up in Moravská Ostrava, and the Polana branch would have the right to nominate two members. And why had Polana not yet sent in members' subscriptions?

Who would go and live in the *hakhshara*? Who would be the happy one . . . *Hakhshara* meant Palestine. Life, happiness, the fatherland.

Here even non-religious terms took on a mystic note. *Hakhshara!* What a lovely word! This was the very brotherhood of the poor that Leyb Abrahamovich was always talking about. Twenty or twenty-five boys and girls would get together and go out into the wide world (where, oh where was Moravská Ostrava?). In some strange city they would find work, no matter whether it was as bricklayers, factory workers, shop assistants or office messengers, and no matter what the pay, for they all put their wages into a common fund. They would live together, eat together, own their clothes and linen together, for it made sense that the one who was going to look for a job should dress better that day; next morning it would be somebody else's turn to dress to go out. Brothers and sisters. In the evenings and on Sundays the leaders would teach them the principles of the movement, and Hebrew – yes, the language of the prophets, the poets and kings of Israel – was being revived in the new country, too. And then – then would come Palestine.

Who was to go to the *hakhshara*? Directly and by devious ways thirteen of them applied, all of them

75

young except for the family of Srul Nakhamkes, who might go direct without pausing in the *hakhshara*. New alliances were forming and old bitternesses being overcome. Who would be judged by the branch mature enough and worthy to be sent, the very first, in the history of Polana, to have the joy of seeing the promised land?

It was not only the *halutz* Zionists who were excited about these questions. The whole village was in a ferment. The doubters among the *mizrakhi* members were asking, wide-eyed: Is it really true? And beginning to be sorry they had had khaki blouses made with the yellow Star of David on the sleeve, blouses that Solomon Fuchs was not yet asking them to pay for simply because in the winter there would be a *mizrakhi* dance at the Fuchses' place. What comparison could there be, though, between a dance and – Palestine?

Sura's friends were sitting about in the Fuchses' shop all morning, on cases of candles or nails and on empty vinegar barrels.

'What can I do for you?' Sura spoke Ruthenian to the customers and weighed up salt and flour for them, poured vinegar and paraffin oil into their bottles, and all the while talked Yiddish to her friends: 'Just you wait and see! First I'd like to know just who is going to Palestine from Polana. Somebody's thought up a new way to get money out of foolish Jews. What are things like in the *hakhshara?* Why don't you ask Hanele Shafar, not me? . . . No,' she went on in Ruthenian to an old woman who was leaning over the counter to whisper softly, 'you know we don't give credit,' and she took the packet of cattle salt she had weighed out off the counter and put it on a shelf behind her. Then she went across to sell nails to a peasant. 'Well, they're going to sleep together,' she smiled, 'at least they won't have anything to be afraid of, will they? . . . Two pence more,' she said to the customer. 'They say Shloym Katz is going as well. As for the Sabbath, of course the factories in Ostrava keep the Sabbath . . . Yes, that's right, I thought you'd find the change . . .' she smiled at the old woman and handed the packet over. 'And of course they'll only eat *kosher* food.'

The longing to escape from the greyness of this existence, the longing for life and a scrap of happiness – and all that was contained in the word 'Palestine' – inspired Hanele, too. One sunny autumn morning, when the leaves were beginning to fall, bent over the wash-tub in the garden, in no more than a skirt, a blouse and shoes on her bare feet, Hanele explained to her mother as she stood there breaking dry branches off the apple-tree to feed the fire under the boiler on the grass.

Mother shot upright with her arms full of dry twigs, and looked at her daughter. 'You must be mad.'

'I'm not, Mother. If they let me go, I'm going to ask Etelka to lend me the money and then I'll be off to Palestine.'

'You really are mad, my girl.'

Hanele bent over the wash-board. Wavy locks of hair fell across her face.

'Who else is going?' asked her mother sternly. She wanted to hear the name of Shloym Katz.

'I don't know, it hasn't been decided yet. It might be young Eizigovich.'

Pinches Yakubovich chose this moment to come and see them in the orchard. Sitting down on the edge of a wooden pail full of damp washing, he watched the flames licking ruddily at the bottom of the boiler, and listened to the two women. There were few things in Polana that were not discussed openly in front of the whole congregation, and they were used to Pinches turning up and sitting with them for a while, saying little and then going away again.

They went on with their conversation as they worked. They were both a little irritated.

Pinches Yakubovich sat there watching them. He looked at Hanele. Yet what he saw was not her red face, so pretty at that moment, nor her bare arms, nor the breasts shaking beneath her blouse as she worked. He was looking right into her soul, and his spirit saw a great light all at once, as if rain-clouds had parted and the sun was shining through on the pastures and the feeding flocks. In a flash he realised that he was one of the elect, after all; just when he had almost forgotten how to speak, he found the words coming of their own accord: 'Once upon a time, long, long ago, there lived a Jew in Cracow . . .'

'Oh, Pinches, you and your fairy-tales!' said Hanele without lifting her eyes from her wash-board.

'. . . and the angel of dreams came to him one day. The angel said: "If you follow the setting sun you will come to a city that is called Prague. Through that city there flows a river called Vltava and across the river

78

there is a stone bridge. You will find treasures of gold hidden there. Set off at once!" In the morning the Jew woke up and thought to himself: Well, what is a dream? Then the following night the angel of dreams appeared again and said the same words to him. When the same thing happened the third night, the Jew realised that his dream was sent by God and so he set off on his journey. He found Prague and the Vltava and the stone bridge. He walked about by the bridge, over the bridge, on the other side of the bridge, looking all over the place and searching the ground; suddenly two soldiers caught hold of him from behind. "Look, a stinking Jew! Spying for the enemy, are you? Just you wait!" He begged and prayed in vain; they took him off to the bridge tower where their commander sat. "A spy? Hang him!" said the officer. Again he begged and prayed and swore he was no spy. In the end there was nothing for it but to tell the whole story of his dream. The officer laughed fit to burst. "Oh, you fool of a Jew! Believing in dreams! If I believed in dreams, now, I'd have hurried to Cracow this very day. Last night I dreamed I was in the house of a certain Jew there, I even remember what he was called," and he gave the prisoner's name, "I even re-member what his house looked like," and he described the prisoner's own home, "and I dreamed I found a treasure in his stove." He felt so happy about it that he let the Jew go. He thanked his benefactor and set off back home to Cracow. At home he had barely taken the first brick out of the stove wall and there was the treasure of gold. Valuable treasure worth a great deal of money . . . That was the story the rabbi told his disciples. When he had finished he said: "Why have I told you this story? So you might know that we are all in search of something. Sooner or later we all find it, but not far away among strangers. At home. In our own hearts. And in our souls."'

When the girl is arguing with her mother for her right to go out into the world, when she is composing in her mind a letter asking her sister for help, and when she is thinking up little tricks to make sure it is she who is chosen, then it is inevitable that a fairy-tale will end, just as the yellow leaves of the apple-tree fall through the clear air and drop into the suds frothing around her knuckles. Unless the tale has been told for the satisfaction of the teller alone.

That night in bed Hanele's parents talked about her for a long time. There were many reasons for saying 'No!' firmly, not simply that they would be left alone – the thought of which made her mother cry, for it is the lot of parents to grow old and be left alone. On the other hand, Hanele would be twenty-one next winter. Would Etelka or Bálinka be able to find her a husband, these days, when nobody was interested in anything but money? What could her sisters give her? They might contribute to her bottom drawer, at most. Would she find a husband in the village? Shloym Katz? Shame!

At last Father found a way out, one that suited his nature: the golden compromise. She could go to Moravská Ostrava, but not to Palestine. That would ease her mother's anxieties too. Perhaps after all she would find someone in Ostrava.

Next morning Joseph Shafar spoke to his daughter: 'Mother and I have talked it over. We don't promise anything, but we may let you go to Moravská Ostrava. It will depend on who else is going with you, and who you will be staying with when you get there.' (Oh, yes, Hanele knew well enough what he meant!) 'First, though, you must give me your oath,' he said sternly, 'that you will find a job with a Jewish gentleman, that you will keep the Sabbath and never let unclean food pass your lips.'

He did not wait to hear Hanele's oath. The stern tone was more in the nature of proof that he had been a right-thinking father, when the time came to bear witness before the Judgement Seat.

It was, of course, not young Eizigovich who had the best chance of being elected to join the *hakhshara*, but Shloym Katz, the conscientious, hard-working secretary of the branch. And Hanele knew that, at the next meeting, if she went out into the yard and waited for a moment by the pile of winter firing, Shloym would soon follow her out.

'Hanele!' he caught hold of her hand. 'Why were you so unkind to me last time?'

'Shloym, dear, you know perfectly well you mustn't kiss me the way you did.' She stroked his cheek. 'I wanted to say something else, though, now. Which of the girls will be going?'

'We don't know yet.'

'Couldn't I go?'

'You, Hanele?' he cried happily. Then he thought about it. 'I think it could be you, if I spoke to some of

81

them about it.' Then he suddenly realised that Hanele's words were really the answer to his question of the previous evening. A great joy overwhelmed him. Taking the girl in his arms he gazed at her, his face close to hers. Hanele could see the lights dancing in his eyes. 'Hanele! My happiness! You understood me and you haven't forgotten?' His voice broke. Then the lights in his eyes became flames and the flames leaped. 'With me? . . . With me!' He kissed Hanele, wildly, like he had tried to kiss her the time before. And she did not put up much resistance this time.

'That was what I wanted to talk to you about, Shloym,' she said as she freed herself. She was blushing and her eyes were cast down; one foot rubbed up and down against the pile of firewood. 'You see, Shloym, . . . I wanted to ask a favour of you . . . It's like this, Shloym . . . if you go, my parents won't let me go. Shloym, do you think . . . would you wait and go to the next *hakhshara*?'

He had expected her to say something quite different and was brought up short.

'I would wait for you there . . .'

Shloym was looking at the ground and thinking hard. His brow was furrowed. Then he reached a sudden decision and took the girl's hands. 'Do you love me, Hanele?'

'Why shouldn't I be fond of you, Shloym?'

'No,' he said and embraced her again, 'say more than that.'

'I love you, Shloym,' and she kissed him on the cheek.

'I would do anything in the world for you, Hanele.'

The meeting charged Shloym to write to Prague again. There were still things they wanted to know; a number of points were still not clear. When you are deciding the whole of your future you cannot be irresponsible.

'When the answer comes, we'll elect who's to go,' declared the chairman, Leyb Abrahamovich.

The excitement! Who would be the two chosen to go? You who have been listening to your chairman in such silence that you could hear Abrahamovich's wife's needle going in and out of the children's trousers she was mending, make the best of the few days that still remain, start campaigning, persuade people, beg, promise, threaten, undermine authority, set up groups, lay bare evils, learn the ABC of political life, for now the whole of your future is at stake! Hannah Shafar, strain your strength to its utmost, your happiness hangs in the balance!

The virgin forests of Polana are far away from the world, further away from Prague than any other point in Europe. On the second or third day a letter from Prague will arrive at the railway station, on the fourth day a trap will come from the town to fetch it, on the fifth day a peasant trap will take it over the hills to the village on the other side, and on the sixth or the eighth day the Polana parish messenger will come for it; he only comes three times a week. If everything goes well, though, you can expect an answer in a fortnight. There's no hurry.

It took longer than that. But it came.

83

The trouble was, the messenger brought the answer on a Friday, and because he lingered on the way, there were not just three, but a host of stars in the sky by the time he arrived. At that time Leyb Abrahamovich was standing before the tabernacle in the synagogue, the only one wearing his black and white striped *tallith*, and so he called out in a magnificent voice, straining his vocal chords to their utmost, the great sevenfold refrain: '*Rititi! Tarara!* Come, my friend, to meet the Bride!' And Leyb's wife, who was just lighting the Sabbath candles, accepted the letter with annoyance, as once again it would mean some meeting or other, and a dirty floor, which she'd only just scrubbed clean this afternoon, and she threw it down on her husband's cobbler's bench.

When Leyb came home and said '*Gut shabos!*' he could not read it as it was now the Sabbath and work was no longer permitted.

News of the arrival of the letter from Prague spread throughout Polana. Yet it lay there unopened all through Friday evening and all day Saturday on the bench among the pliers, the awls, the cobbler's thread, the tin of glue and the bits of glass he used for scraping the leather; his cobbler's hammer weighted it down. People kept coming to look at it and tried to pretend their smiles of excitement were smiles of amusement.

There were even those who thought up ways of deceiving the Lord their God: Why not open the letter? Is it not fitting to read pious things on the Sabbath? Of course it is. And is not the promised land a most fitting thing that finds favour in the sight of the Lord?

Leyb Abrahamovich stretched out his hand, palm raised, in the direction of the letter, thus fending off temptation: 'Everything in its own good time!'

This evening it will be settled . . . This evening the elections will be held!

Excitement now reached fever pitch. At the last moment the candidates were running about the village to remind their friends of promised votes. So was Hanele. Father and Mother would be going with her that evening; they had joined the organisation as well, as their business was reviving and their child needed their help.

From the half-cold Sabbath dinner, kept from the day before in the cooling bread oven, to the moment when the Lord sends His three stars to call the Sabbath Queen back to His throne, it is always a long time. Married couples usually spend the time in bed, for during that time nothing that resembles work may be done. The young people, dressed in their best, parade up and down the road to the forester's cottage. But what can you do on a long autumn evening when you are not allowed to light the lamps, and the minutes drag by?

Hanele, all excited, kept running out on to the balcony to see whether the three stars had appeared, or in fact to see whether the third had appeared, for Father did not see or at least did not recognise as real the one that was twinkling from time to time in the clouds above Menshul. At last the third, indubitable one came out. Mother lit the first weekday light, set the lamp alight, and then the Shafars, like all the other families, could proceed to the ceremony of *havduleh*.*

Hanele, the youngest member of the family, holds high above her head a lighted taper of six plaited strands and five flames; her father has at his right hand a glass of spirits, at his left a flask of cloves and sweet spices; he prays over them and he prays over the light. He takes a deep look into the glass, then unstoppers the flask and sniffs the spices, so that he may not forget in the week to come what the promised land smells like. Then he spills a little of the spirits on the table, takes the taper from Hanele's hands, and sets the libation alight. He dips his fingers into the blue flame and draws them across his brow that his thoughts may be clear, across his heart that it may be kind, across his neck that it may be strong, and round the inside of his pockets that . . . Is that business with the pockets going to be any good, when it has never been any good, all the times it has been performed before at the departure of the Queen of the Sabbath? . . . Oh, yes, it might help this time, it really might; a little bit, anyway . . . But it did not help. Father just had not got the lucky touch.

'*Gute woch!*' all the families in Polana were wishing each other.

'Hurry up, Father, hurry up, Mother,' Hanele was impatient.

The *halutz* supporters were streaming through the darkness to Abrahamovich's cottage. The room was crowded. Up on the stove the children did not have enough room to move.

They all fell silent as Leyb Abrahamovich got to his feet. The sound of his cobbler's knife slitting the enve-lope was like the sword of the Archangel slashing

86

through the air. Leyb Abrahamovich took out the letter, unfolded it, and solemnly handed it over to Shloym Katz, who was a fluent reader. The silence was impressive. Hanele's heart was beating hard.

The letter was long and matter-of-fact: the Palestine Committee had complained that emigrants sent from Sub-Carpathian Ruthenia were the least qualified of all the workers sent to Palestine, the least capable and also the least efficient. It was therefore necessary to choose members for the *hakhshara* most carefully and most conscientiously. Reports from Palestine showed that the following were welcome there: trained farmers, carpenters and cabinet-makers, bricklayers, plasterers, smiths (Oh, Srul Nakhamkes felt as though someone had poured out sweet wine and now it was flowing through his body!), locksmiths, mechanics, tool-makers and masseurs. There were too many tailors and dressmakers, too many cobblers (the small space of cheek that was visible below Leyb Abrahamovich's eyes blushed darkly), glaziers, barbers, hairdressers and dentists, and people of these trades were not welcome. With reference to the *hakhshara* being set up in Moravská Ostrava, every new member was required to pay his own fare there and bring with him two sets of clothing (Ooo!), two sets of underwear, two pairs of shoes, a pillow and a bedcover (Oy! vey!). Communal quarters would be provided, and work would be found for the members of the *hakhshara* in factories and workshops in Greater Ostrava. All wages, however high, would be put into the common fund, which would pay for the communal canteen, washing and cleaning; men who smoked would

87

be given three crowns a week for cigarettes, and women one crown for postage stamps. Whatever was left would be paid into the Palestine Fund. (Oy! vey!). The *hakhshara* would last at least eight months. Every evening and every holiday morning as well, the leader of the *hakhshara*, who must be unconditionally obeyed, would teach Hebrew and Zionist ideology. At the end of that time examinations would be held, and those whom the examiners found physically and mentally fit would be added to the list of those who could emigrate to Palestine when emigration certificates were granted by the Palestine Committee of Great Britain. The journey to Palestine would cost 1,500 crowns and each emigrant would be required to find this money himself (Oyoyoy . . . oyoy!). 'We must point out most emphatically that it is absolutely inadmissible for branches to be as slow in sending in membership contributions as is the Polana branch, and warn them that, unless the money due for registration fees and membership stamps is received at once, we shall be forced to cite the Polana branch in the Zionist paper.'

The promised land of their fathers disappeared in the far distance, and the scents of Palestine, carefully preserved in stoppered flasks and sniffed at but half an hour before with such piety, dissolved in the sweaty smell of the cobbler's shop.

The Polana Jews sat there and stood there motionless, and the last sighs emerged from their lungs like the air squeezed out of a balloon: Oyoyoy. But it was soft and inaudible.

Leyb Abrahamovich's leonine face did not look at all triumphant, and his wandering eyes had lost their gleam of leadership, as he asked in a voice that betrayed a quivering heart: 'Who will stand for election to the *hakhshara?*'

No one. The silence exuded a chill.

'The end of the *halutz* movement . . . The end of leadership . . . The end of Polana,' went round and round in Leyb Abrahamovich's dulled mind.

Then a clear voice suddenly broke the silence: 'I will.'

It was the voice of Hanele Shafar. They all turned in the direction of the voice. May you be blessed, for you have saved a great thing!

Oh! What a silver sound that voice had for Leyb Abrahamovich! No bell rung to announce to the besieged that help is drawing nigh ever tinkled so clearly in the morning mists. May the Lord reward her. The spirit of the leader, coiled deep in a trench in the ground, shot up and rushed out at the gates, brandishing a sword on high.

'Hanele Shafar come forward,' Leyb Abrahamovich cried in a great voice. 'Who is for her?'

Everybody!

'Is there anyone against?' and his voice and his searching eyes were ready in advance to crush anyone who might dare, and his bristling beard was terrible to behold.

'No one.'

'Hanele Shafar is elected.'

Hanele, the heroine of the evening, the target for praise and hatred in days to come, stood up straight for all to admire, blushing, smiling, and her heart beating like a drum-roll.

Hanele Shafar's fate is sealed – for life.

Next morning the packing-cases and barrels in the Fuchses' shop were more in request than ever, and some of Sura's friends had to stand about and lean against the counters. They were laughing and joking. What fun! What a triumph! The cobbler was finished and done for. What a joke!

Sura divided her smiling attention between her friends and her professional duties. 'No, we do not give goods on credit and Father does not need any work done at the moment,' she said to a Ruthenian lumberman with a polite smile. 'Why don't you go to your co-op, or to the Shafars'? They might give you credit there. What did I tell you?' she went on in Yiddish. 'There's nobody going. Except Hanele Shafar. Hannah knows what she's doing. If you've got nothing to offer you've got to take steps yourself as long as you're young and pretty enough, and the gentlemen of Ostrava are certainly dying with expectation, waiting for brides to appear for them from Polana. Father is not in,' she turned back to the lumberman. 'No, I don't know when he'll be back, but he won't let you have anything on credit, either . . . The fools! They thought they were going to get a trip to Ostrava and on to Palestine, free and for nothing. Weren't they surprised, yesterday, to hear they'd got to work in Ostrava for nothing for eight months! Didn't I say all along it was just a trick to get money out of people? They didn't even realise they'd got to pay membership fees.'

Sura was laughing as she put a package in front of a Ruthenian woman and said: 'No, we don't give sweets free . . . Mr Shafar always gives you a bag of sweets for the children? Really? Well, we can't let ourselves be put to shame, can we? But you'll have to give me the parcel back for a minute. I'll give you poorer quality, that'll make three crowns; or else I'll cheat you out of two crowns on the weight, and then I'll be able to give you fifty hellers' worth of sweets for nothing . . . You don't want that? There you are, you see! . . . What can I do for you?' and she stuffed a big piece of soft-centred chocolate into her mouth as she turned to the next customer. 'What are all those secretaries going to live on, walking about Prague and doing nothing? Perhaps they thought somebody was going to teach them He-brew and those politics of theirs for *gemilut khasadim?* What about the green collecting boxes they hung up by their beds,' she gave a smile, 'to throw a penny in for every kiss – did they think those were free too? It's no good your waiting,' she said in Ruthenian, 'Father is not in and he won't be in for a long time . . . Now just listen to me: in six months it'll be all over, Leyb Abra-hamovich will be left all alone, and the village will settle down again . . . Yoy! I haven't told you the best thing, yet: the others can't afford it, but do you know why Shloym Katz isn't going? The rabbi sent word to old Katz that if he lent Shloym money for the journey, and if Shloym didn't stop his nonsense anyway, the old man's begging licence would be taken off him . . .'

The friends burst out laughing. 'Who brought the message?'

'Who brought him the message? Does it matter who brought him the message?'

Hanele had been living in Ostrava for two months.

Before day broke on that fateful morning, when they lit the kitchen lamp and Hanele was waiting for the cart to take her and her box to the railway station, and Mother was wiping away tears, Father came up to Hanele, and though he was a man of few words, who never spoke to his daughter but of the most ordinary matters, he said: 'I am not good at talking, but if your Grandfather were alive he would say: Never forget that you are a daughter of Israel. When you meet with *goyim*, however great and powerful, however wealthy they may be, even the nobility, pay them the respect that is their due but never forget that you are more than they, that you are a Jewess, that you are a king's daughter, that you acknowledge no lord but the Lord thy God. Grandfather would have found finer words but that's the best I can do.'

Ostrava! Košice was a nicer town. Even the snow didn't fall properly in Ostrava, it was black and turned to mud. Still, there were new buildings, electric lights, wonderful shop windows, crowds of people, and all that was lovely to look at.

She was in Ostrava. Or rather, she had got away from the emptiness of Polana, and her promises to Shloym and his unwelcome attentions were far behind her. He had become a nuisance and had reproached her because of his father. 'That's why you don't want me, isn't it?' he said, and she could see the angry fire in his eyes and the furious look on his grim face. It was not only because of his father, though . . . That night had not been a nice experience, and Hanele did not like thinking of it. No, she was not firmly rooted in Ostrava. Polana still came into her mind too much.

The *hakhshara* was neither as wonderful as Leyb Abrahamovich had painted it, nor as bad as Sura Fuchs had depicted. The *kedma** was a six-roomed house in Mariánské Hory, with a garden where they grew potatoes. There were twenty-six boys and twelve girls there, and six permanent paid workers as well, who lived and ate with them. 'Those are the real Zionists,' Joey Taussig declared of them; he had been given a job as an errand boy, spoke nothing but Czech and knew all the latest jokes. 'Don't you know what a Zionist is? A Jew who uses another Jew's money to send a third Jew to Palestine.' They were all at work during the day, and in the evenings and on Sundays they either had lessons or held meetings. Hanele did not like these meetings much, and the 'criticism meetings' she did not like at all; the envious boys flushed with passion, would attack one another furiously for holding the wrong views and not upholding the right principles, and the girls would try to cover up their jealousies in mutual reproaches about untidiness in the bedrooms and bathroom, clothes left lying about, litter on the floor and rough ways; there were times when the shouting and weeping went on until the small hours. The food was good, but everything was not *kosher*. True, out and out unclean foods like

93

pork were never served, and the order of serving meat and milk dishes was kept to, but all kinds of things were *treyfe,** like the milk; you could be sure the milker had not washed his hands under running spring water and dipped them in bran before milking. The principle of communal ownership of clothes and linen was not absolutely adhered to either. But the life was tolerable. Joey Taussig was always trying to pat her in the corridors and giggling; Paul Hartstein pestered her a bit, too, and Selma Stránská, who slept next to her in the girls' room, was a nasty quarrelsome creature; but in spite of it all, the bustle and excitement of the life were much, much nicer than the quiet of Polana.

Hanele was sent to work for the firm of Roubiček and Löbl and so Father could be satisfied on that score. She did not put in her letters that the firm worked on the Sabbath, and Father was careful never to ask. It was a workshop where they made travelling bags and rucksacks, and for the work Hanele did sewing on the straps 'Roubiček and Löbl' paid the *kedma* 60 crowns a week. All she got of it was fifty hellers for a postage stamp and one franked postcard bearing a Zionist slogan, and because the factory was a long way off, and she could not have gone back to Mariánské Hory for dinner, she was also given 2.50 crowns a day for her midday meal. She liked working in the factory. It was clean, pleasant work; she had been used to much harder jobs. The girls who worked at the sewing machines with her, Christians, were friendly and cheerful, and Hanele was fond of fun and laughter. All day long they talked about the movies and their boyfriends.

'What about you, Hanichka? You never say anything about boys. Are you a Jewish nun, or something?' they used to tease her. How strange it sounded when they called her 'Hanichka' or 'Anna'.*

Hanele laughed. What could she have told them about? There was one incident, though. She could have told them about that ugly night in the orchard. About the thing she carried about inside her and with her everywhere, the thing she dreamed about, and when she was roused from her dream in the night (why could she not hear Grandfather's mills?) she did not know where she was and her forehead was covered in perspiration. But that was something she would never have revealed to a living soul.

Although Shloym Katz pressed him, Leyb Abrahamovich had refused to call another *halutz* meeting before Hanele left. Perhaps he feared a repetition of the previous meeting; the next one, alas, might be less successful. This purely political consideration was not without its effect on the purely private feelings of the branch secretary: Shloym had no opportunity of seeing Hanele. He did his best to find one, however, and was prepared to press hard for it. At first it all seemed very innocent; several times a day he would turn up at the shop to purchase some trifle, and exchange a few words with the girl in the presence of her mother, for Mother was always there. Hanele did not mind being under such close watch, though, for she had begun to be a little afraid of Shloym. Then he started writing her notes and giving them to Ruthenian children to bring to her, and that was not only very unpleasant, but even dangerous.

95

He wanted to see her, he wrote, he had got to see her even if he paid for it with his life. She did not answer. He wrote again a few days before the day she was due to leave, and the tone of his letters showed how serious his distress was. 'I cannot live without you. Unless you let me see you something terrible will happen. I do not know what, but it will be something dreadful.'

Two days before she left she noticed something moving every now and again, behind the cottages on the other side of the road and beyond their garden fences, ever since morning. It was about three hundred paces away from the Shafars', at a point where the house could be easily seen. Hanele guessed that the head that kept popping up behind the potatoes was Shloym's. She grew very uneasy. Shloym waited there from early morning almost until midday. Father had gone into the village on some errand, and when Mother went out into the farmyard for a moment Hanele saw Shloym jump over the fence, dash across the gardens and into the shop and right through into the house. He was deathly pale. He flashed his eyes at her and gasped in a breathless voice: 'The last two nights before you leave I'm going to wait in the orchard for you to come out, from evening until the next morning – whether you come or not. I know now what terrible thing is going to happen.' Then he dashed out again. What a dreadful idea! The things he thought of! Of course she would not go anywhere. It was obvious she wouldn't.

That evening, when her parents had gone to bed and were asleep in the next room, her nerves could only bear the thought of him waiting there for an hour, or at most, two. She got up and saw him through the window. Then she lay down and tossed on the bed again, burying her head in the pillow, feeling angry and tearful in turn. No, she would not go out! In the end she went, of course. Just for a moment, she would be back straightaway, she would just tell him off and send him packing. She slipped slippers on her bare feet and flung an old coat over her nightdress.

He would not listen to reason, though. Before she left he wanted her to give her solemn promise that she would marry him. It was no use trying to talk sensibly to him. All her excuses and prevarications and references to the future drew from him unseemly talk; he kept on insisting and when she finally said obstinately, 'No, then!' he smothered her in passionate reproaches, reproaching her for holding his father against him, reproaching her for letting him down and deceiving him, making it impossible for him to go to Palestine, and ruining his life. He was trembling from head to foot. Then he tried to kiss her. She resisted. He made a rush at her, she dug her fingers into his eye sockets and pushed his head away; he struggled with her, tearing all the buttons off her coat, holding her in his arms almost naked. When she bit his hand and managed to escape he caught up with her by an apple tree and shook her so hard her head kept knocking against the tree trunk. It was all the more horrible because this struggle was having to be carried on under the stars without a sound, because her parents were sleeping just beyond the window there. Then he fell at her feet and embraced her knees and broke into torrents of tears. She was exhausted, and when he got to his feet and begged her forgiveness and her pity in a sad whisper, she could no longer resist his kisses. She wept with him. She was sorry for him. They stood there kissing and trembling with excitement and cold.

Why should Polana keep coming back and mingling with Ostrava? . . . Shloym had written to her three times, and once she had sent him a postcard out of her weekly ration, with a greeting. He could not live without her, he had to see her, even if it meant his death, and if he could not find the money for the journey he would set out for Ostrava on foot! Hanele did not want him to come and see her, she did not want him to write to her. Why could he not leave her alone in this new life she had found? Polana, Polana still kept its hold on her! . . . What would happen if he came? At home there were her parents she could confess to. Who would protect her from him here? . . . Joey Taussig, or Paul Hartstein?

Hanele washed her hands at work, put on her coat and went out for dinner. She had only an hour, and the milk bar was quite a way.

As she went along she noticed a Jew standing at the corner of the street. He was nicely dressed, tall and well-shaven, but even so his face looked as dark as a smith's. And he had a big nose. He might have been thirty-two or three. He was looking at her as she came towards him; looking at her with pleasure but not obtrusively. A lot of people found Hanele nice to look at and often turned to look at her; she was quite aware of this.

As she passed him, though, the stranger smiled at her, a nice smile revealing big teeth, and said: 'Slovakia or Ruthenia?'

Hanele was used to answering strangers politely, from the shop and the tap-room at home. 'Ruthenia.'

The stranger was now walking by her side. 'What are they doing there these days? My name is Ivo Karajich. You don't mind if I go a little way with you, do you? Are they still waiting for the Messiah?'

'Of course,' she said wonderingly, and looked up at him. What a nose! She had never seen a nose like that before. She smiled, the way you smile at a close acquaintance you haven't seen for some time and suddenly notice that they are terribly fat or have a funny beard. No, he was not good-looking; it was only from a distance that he gave that impression, but he had kind eyes and a nice smile.

'When is He going to come?' he asked.

'The Svalava rabbi dreamed that He was going to come this spring.'

His lips bent a little as though he wanted to laugh, but the smile disappeared again. He gazed into her face and his head seemed to be shaking ever so slightly, as if to say 'Terrible!' And then it stopped shaking and he just went on gazing.

'Lots of people have told you what lovely eyes you have, haven't they? Are you a *halutz* Zionist or a *betarka*?'*

'*Halutz*'.

'Two Messiahs all at once, then! The old and the new.'

'What do you mean?'

'Surely it's the same thing, the Messiah and Palestine?' he said half in jest and half in earnest. 'Illusions again.'

99

'What are illusions?'

He laughed outright, showing his fine white teeth. 'You're quite right, I'm mad. That's what Mother says, too. I really wanted to say something quite different, though – to ask a favour of you. You don't seem to be expecting anyone and I am on my own. Will you allow me to go on looking at you for a while? And it would be very nice if you would accept an invitation to have dinner with me.'

Hanele was not prepared for that.

'All right,' she said shyly before she had time to consider how to answer.

'That is kind of you. Thank you. We can talk about Ruthenia.'

'I'd rather talk about Ostrava.' She did not want to have to think of Polana. 'But won't the food be *treyfe*?' she asked, looking up at him.

'Oh, of course, I forgot,' he smiled at her. 'We'll order something that can't not be *kosher*, and tell them not to give us milk spoons to eat our meat with.'

He took her up to a restaurant frequented by commercial travellers and unmarried clerks from the civil service and works' offices, where they stick a duplicated menu in the window showing the prices. Through the plate-glass window she saw the tables laid ready, vases of artificial flowers on them, ornate lights, a waiter helping a customer out of his overcoat; then she remembered that under her coat she was wearing a blouse which would do for Polana but not here.

'I can't go in there.'

He joked with her and explained everything on the menu and tried to persuade her, but she was insistent.

'Where do you usually go?'

'To the milk bar.'

So they went to the milk bar. He brought her cream cakes and apple tart. Sitting by her side he drank a glass of milk and spoke a lot about all kinds of things, gazed at her and asked her many questions about Polana, about the *hakhshara*, about all she had seen during those two months. Then he brought her more to eat and they laughed together. Hanele watched the round-faced clock on the wall of the milk bar and was surprised to see how the minutes had flown past.

When he paid the bill Ivo Karajich picked up a ten-crown piece in his fingertips, said 'Changer passer hey presto!' and snapped his fingers and the ten-crown piece was gone. Then he put it in his left hand and shut his fingers over it, saying 'Mumbo Jumbo!' and the left hand was empty and the coin in the right hand again.

'Just look at the things a commercial traveller's got to learn to do!'

He laughed with her, a hearty boyish laugh; why did people at home never really laugh?

They stayed to the very last minute. Then together they ran towards the factory, still laughing.

That was how it all began. Hanele remembers every word that was spoken during that hour.

*

'. . . For treachery, for keeping company with the direst enemies of Israel, for gross breach of discipline and for immoral living, Hannah Shafar is expelled from the *kedma*. Her local branch will be informed of this decision.'

This was the conclusion of the accusation read out by the chairman of the *hakhshara* at one of the criticism meetings. The boys listened to the sentence calmly, as if it was the only reasonable decision to take, but the girls clapped stormily and Selma Stránská called out: 'Hear! Hear!'

Hanele had never liked those criticism meetings. Fortunately she was not present on this occasion.

'But that's the problem!' the secretary of the *kedma* added. 'Inform her local branch! She hasn't got one.'

'That's not possible. Who sent her here in the first place?' the chairman asked sternly.

'The central office wrote to them four times and they never answered; like throwing the letters to the winds. They did not pay for membership stamps and they didn't return them either, they didn't pay for membership cards and they didn't return them either, they didn't send in any money from the collecting boxes and they didn't return the boxes either. If only they had shown some sign of life! They might at least have put salt in the boxes!' Joey Taussig laughed. 'Twice the Polana branch was cited in the paper as a warning to them, and then they were crossed off the list . . . Wait a minute, it's no laughing matter! There's another thing: a letter came for the Shafar girl today. Shall I send it on to her?'

'No!' the chairman shouted. 'Send it back!'

'All right. Polana, Shloym Katz, that's it.'

Hanele was not living in the *kedma* any longer. Nor was she sewing straps on rucksacks for the firm of Roubiček and Löbl. She was sitting in the editorial office of *The Free Thinker* and living in a nice furnished room for which she paid thirty crowns a week. The change was effected very quickly. One day she simply did not go back to the *kedma*, and the next morning Mr Karajich sent a messenger for Hanele's things, from the wholesale enamelware firm for whom he travelled. It was settled. The job was also found for her by Mr Karajich. He was the secretary of 'Free Thinking', the chairman of the Cremation Society and a member of the editorial board of *The Free Thinker*. And now Hanele, together with Mr Pšenička, an elderly gentleman whose long-stemmed pipe troubled her a great deal, formed the office staff of all three legal bodies together.

There is no denying that the leaps and bounds made by Hanele were great indeed. From Polana to the *kedma* to *The Free Thinker* – all in ten weeks; it was almost too much.

What? . . . Dead *goyim* are burned here? Don't pull my leg . . . In a furnace? . . . What? Jews as well?

What is the real truth? Aren't there any Jews here in Ostrava? Are there only Jews in Polana and then a few in Košice and then no more anywhere else? What is the truth, then? What sort of Jews do you call them if they haven't their own tongue and talk *goy* even to each other and dress like *goyim* and do not keep the Sabbath, if they eat *treyfe* food and don't pray and don't do any of the

103

things that make a Jew a Jew? And then let themselves be burned in furnaces?

'And really, young lady,' Mr Pšenička instructed her, 'they might at least have taught you this much in the Czech school you went to back there: Jew is not written as a noun, but as the adjective Jewish, and the word Jewish is not used at all, so you must fill in the column "religion" with the word "Israelite", and then you don't write it like that at all, you just put "Is".'

'What does Mr Karajich do at the burning?'

'Makes speeches.'

'What kind?'

'Well, you know, he generally tells people what to do.'

'What, for instance?'

'Well, he tells them not to believe clergymen and monsters of that kind. Christian or Jewish. One as bad as the other.'

When he was not away travelling, Ivo Karajich would drop in at the editorial office at midday or just after five. He would smile and display his beautiful teeth.

'How are you, Hanichka . . . Come and have dinner with me today . . . Wouldn't you like to go to the pictures with me, Anna?'

He took her to the cinema. Once he took her to the theatre. After the film and after the theatre they would go and sit in a café where a band was playing and everything was gilt and there were lots of lights. Hanele had never been inside a cinema before. She had never seen a play. Or even heard a concert. Only once had she seen a café all lit up, in Košice, and then only from the street.

Oyoy! How far away Polana seemed now!

Ivo Karajich rarely talked of serious matters with her. And then only in passing.

'Do drop those Polana ideas, Hanichka,' he said once, half joking and half in earnest, as they sat in the café. 'There is no Lord God, there is no promised land, there are no Christians and no Jews.'

The world is a strange place, thought Hanele, people seem to be going mad. The Lord God forbids you to go to Palestine, the Lord God commands you to go to Palestine, there is no Lord God, there is no Palestine, the world turns round and round and your heart's treasure is somewhere near a Prague bridge. What is the real truth?

Is it true, then, that God still exists at home in Polana, and here in the west He does not? Was He never here, or did He use to be here and now is here no longer? One thing is sure: in Polana God exists! Who can explain it all to her? Grandfather would have explained it to her, he knew all about everything. Only she could no longer ask Grandfather.

In the rush of those few weeks thoughts like these troubled Hanele. They just troubled her, for it would be going too far to say she really thought these things through. It was the men's business to discuss things like that at criticism meetings.

'What do you mean,' she had said that evening in the café, 'saying there are no Christians and no Jews?'

'Look, Hanichka, that was the way it used to be, but it isn't like that any more. Now the Jews have got equality with the Christians and there is simply no difference between them.'

'You mean we are the same as the Christians?'

'Of course, my dear, for the last fifty years or more. That feeling of inferiority and all the other things that spring from it have got to disappear.'

'You mean the *goyim* are our equals?' Hanele was thinking so hard her forehead wrinkled.

'Oh, I see what the trouble is . . .' Ivo Karajich said slowly, as though it was gradually sinking in, then he clasped his head in his hands and his lips began to smile broadly until suddenly he exploded. Out loud. Laughing loudly and uncontrollably. He laughed so madly that people sitting near turned to look at him. 'Hanele, that's absolutely marvellous!' He was so delighted that he held his head in his hands and swayed from side to side.

'It's the best joke I've heard this year . . . The whole world has accepted Polana on equal terms, and now it's Polana that still hasn't made up its mind to accept the rest of the world as its equal! . . . So that's how it is! . . . Hanichka, you deserve a kiss for that.'

Why doesn't he give me one, then? Hanele thought to herself, and was cross because he was laughing at her. Anyway, why had he never tried to kiss her?

Ivo Karajich was still laughing. Then he suddenly realised that the girl was blushing in confusion and that her eyes were ready to fill with tears.

'Hanichka . . .' he made a gesture as if to stroke her hand, but it was only a breath of air that fluttered over it. '. . . Hanichka . . . don't be angry . . . Believe me, I only wish you well.'

Then came the trip to Prague. A wild, madcap trip, not a single detail of which Hanele would ever forget.

'I've got to pay a visit some distance from here, Hanichka, would you come part of the way with me?' he asked her one Saturday afternoon.

He got the firm's car ready, a little yellow thing with one seat next to the driver's and a big case behind for samples. Somewhat embarrassed, Hanele squeezed herself in.

'Just a little way then. So that I can get a tram back.'

Hanele had never been in a car before, and the ride through Velká Ostrava fascinated her. She would certainly have been a bit scared to drive with anyone else, but Ivo Karajich was at the wheel.

They drove up to the last tram stop.

'Thank you so much, Mr Karajich,' she said enthusiastically, 'it was absolutely wonderful!'

But the car drove on.

'No . . . No . . . Please, Mr Karajich.'

'Just a bit further.'

'No, I can't . . . How shall I get back home?'

'Never mind, Hanichka, we'll go back together.'

'When?'

'Monday morning.'

'You must be mad!' she jumped up in her seat and hit her head against the canvas roof. Karajich laughed and the car raced on.

'Is that the way to speak to your triple boss? Mother says, I'm mad, too, and I love her even more than you.

And that's saying something . . . No, Hanichka, you mustn't pull my sleeve. Look at that cherry tree over there, if we hit it we'll both be in Abraham's bosom . . . It's simply a case of abduction, a textbook case of abduction according to the letter of law, with all the incriminating circumstances.'

'Where are we going?' she asked anxiously.

'To Prague.'

'Pra——?'

The fields powdered with snow ran beside the road, the villages slipped past and the little car seemed to suck in the road like a strip of macaroni.

She did not know whether to burst into angry tears or whether to laugh, and before she could make her mind up they had passed another village.

'I'm only dressed in what I was wearing when I ran out of *The Thinker*,' she said almost crossly.

'Don't worry about that, nobody in Prague will notice,' he smiled as he sat at the wheel.

That little yellow matchbox driving along the roads of north Moravia was certainly no racing car, but in Polana they were accustomed to much slower speeds than those you could get out of the Dub & Arnstein company car, and to Hanele the journey seemed a mad flight. Opava, Bruntal, Šumperk rushed past, it was a pleasure to be moving. On the right were snow-crowned hills, on the left were fields, villages with whitewashed stone cottages quite unlike those she knew, woods which ended almost before you had got properly into them; now and again she got a fright as they turned a corner; then came Hradec where they stopped for a late lunch, Karajich's merry glances and his hand stroking hers; then more fields, plains, more cars overtaking them and fewer hens running across the road, until at last there came in sight the chimneys of the suburbs of Prague. How long could they have been on the road?

It was almost five when they reached the city. The car was put away in a garage and they took the tram to the hotel. Ivo carried his case.

What on earth was this? People in gold-edged caps and a clown at the lift dressed all in red. Hanele would never have dreamed of entering the lift, but she was at their mercy now, and in any case, she was determined to behave nonchalantly, and not show by the merest glance that she was surprised at anything.

In her room he said: 'Wait for me just half an hour, Hanichka. I've got some business to do in town.'

Half an hour later he knocked at her door. He looked stern and official as he stood on the threshold and said: 'We really pay you an awful lot of money for your work in the office, don't we? It must add up to about four hundred and fifty a month. How much do you think you could afford out of that?'

'What for?'

'What for? I'll tell you what for. For a week I've been looking forward to *Carmen* like a child looks forward to a treat and I want to show you the National Theatre. Now I'm not saying you're not nicely dressed, Hanichka, and in your usual good taste, but I know what you're like. The minute you see a woman in a backless gown your Polana pride will make you turn and run, like it did that day you took fright at the paper flowers on the restaurant tables. I think we ought to buy a frock. How much can you afford a month – twenty? thirty?'

She saw through his trick at once. 'No,' she said, and blushed.

'Of course you would say No!' he said crossly. 'That's just like you to spoil my pleasure.'

She went up to him and gave him an affectionate look. She shrugged her shoulders and shook her head gently. 'No, Mr Karajich, you just go by yourself. I'm happy looking through the window at the lights – they are so lovely. I've never seen anything so beautiful. I'll go down and wait for you in the street.'

'Have you gone quite mad?' he cried. 'Do you think this is Ostrava? Haven't you ever heard that the police will arrest any woman who walks about these streets alone, without a man? Hanichka, I swear I'll take an instalment off you every month.'

It turned out that the frock had already arrived. In fact five of them, for her to choose from. And shoes, and a pretty coat. And stockings and a little hat and an evening bag with a hanky and a powder compact and a comb.

'Hurry up, do,' he growled as he went out. 'We haven't got much time.'

How Hanele loved beautiful things! As she looked at them and shook them out and buried her face in them, she said to herself: 'Mad . . . quite mad . . . my mad beloved . . .' and her eyes got quite moist.

How many times did he come and knock on her door and say: 'Ready?' How many times did he stamp about in his room next door and bang on the wall?

Finally she went to him of her own accord.

'Well! . . . Hanichka!' he spoke slowly. His admiration was genuine. 'Well! . . . Hanichka!'

She was pale. Slowly she went up to him. Had she any right to dress in these clothes? Was she not lowering herself in her own eyes? Had she not fallen in his eyes? Did the man before whom she stood dressed like this realise the significance of what she was doing?

A pace away from him she stopped and gazed into his glowing eyes. Something delicate broke in her, as though a gust of wind had broken off a tiny twig. She took the last step forward and kissed his cheek. She swallowed a sob.

He wanted to embrace her but she held him off. Stepping backwards she retreated to the door, slowly, upright as before, and gazing into his eyes with her own wide, dark, beautiful eyes, now filled with tears. As she reached the door and leaned against it the wind rose to its full force and she covered her eyes with her hands, weeping aloud. She felt she was standing there half naked, like that night in the orchard at home, and she felt ashamed. She cried openly and bitterly, like a child.

Ivo went up to her and tried to take her in his arms.

She rebuffed him firmly.

Then, understanding so little of what was happening, he began to shout: 'Shame, Hanichka! . . . Shame on you! Shame on you!'

She forced herself to stand upright, smiled and said: 'Isn't it time we were going to the theatre?'

She walked through the foyer of the National Theatre hanging on Ivo Karajich's arm. Never forget that you are a king's daughter, Grandfather would have said.

111

How silly! As if it were possible to forget what she always carried with her, and as if she needed to remind herself of what was as much a part of her as the blood in her veins! As she mounted the marble staircase, erect and serious, with her dress rustling – a fine dress, but still off-the-peg – as she left her coat in the cloakroom and took her place in the first row of the balcony, laying her handbag in her lap, she did it all as naturally as though she had been there only yesterday.

After the show they had supper in a fashionable place and then went on to a café where a dance band was playing. All evening Ivo's eyes were tender. As they went back to the hotel in a taxi, he kissed her hand several times.

He dropped in at her room for a moment, and did not take his eyes off her as she took off her coat and hat. 'May I smoke here?'

She smiled.

He sat down on the sofa, crossed his legs, and smoked. Then he spoke, saying 'Look here, Hanichka. I made up my mind that if we had a pleasant time here in Prague I would ask you something. Would you have me?'

She grew pale, standing there by the wardrobe. 'What do you mean? I don't understand,' her voice choked.

'Well, just that, altogether, as Mr Pšenička would say, as a husband.'

'I have no dowry.' She said it quietly but resolutely.

'Hmm!' he smiled. 'That is supposed to put me off, is it? Then I'll put you off, too: I am not a Jew.'

'You . . . you . . . aren't a Jew?'

*

112

Ivo Karajich was not in Ostrava. He had been away on a trip for nearly a week and Hanele missed him. True, he wrote every day, sometimes twice; Hanele would slip home for the letters, run her eyes over them, and then in the canteen she would read the slightly sloping, not very legible lines as she ate her soup. At night she took them to bed with her, but the affectionate words written so far away only made her feel lonelier. That was just a week after the miracle of Prague and Ivo!

On Saturday he turned up at *The Free Thinker* at noon. It was really provoking not being able to jump up and call out: 'Ivo!' because Mr Pšenička was there, not to be able to fling her arms impatiently round his neck and take his head in her hands. While everything within her was in a turmoil, all she could do was gaze at him with glowing eyes.

'Put your things on, Hanichka, I want you to do something for me,' he said.

She had to wait until they were outside the door. 'Ivo, my Ivo! I love you, love you, love you so much I'll die!'

He kissed and fondled her. Then they went down into the street together.

'Hanichka!' he began, 'Mother would like to meet you. Go and put your nice white blouse on, and then come and have dinner with us. I'll call for you.'

'I feel a bit scared, Ivo.'

He called for her just before noon. Her heart thumped as they went up the stairs to his flat and he put his key in the door. As they entered the hall a little old lady came to meet them, wearing a white lace cap. Hanele kissed her hand and felt terribly agitated.

The old lady took Hanele into the living room, and the first thing she noticed was a big bookcase.

'That's right, that's Izzie's library. I expect you'll read all those books one day. He's got a lot of nonsense there.'

Hanele blushed a deep red, ashamed to have been caught looking inquisitive. Ivo laughed out loud behind them.

'She doesn't know who Izzie is, Mother.'

'You see, my son imagines,' the old lady went on calmly, 'that I am going to address him by that shocking name Ivo one of these days. He is mistaken.' She inclined her head on one side and looked up at Hanele conspiratorially with bright, clever eyes. 'My son's name is Isaac, you know . . . No? . . . Hasn't he told you?' and the solemn words and dignified nodding of her head made her old lady's eyes look even brighter.

Ivo caught his mother from behind, kissing the white hair where it escaped from the cap, kissing her face and neck, laughing and playing with her like a doll.

'Now leave me alone and don't be a nuisance,' she said gently again.

Sitting Hanele down in an armchair facing the light, the old lady sat on a sofa facing her, Ivo by her side. His right arm was around her shoulder and with his left he held her hand in his, lifting it to his lips to kiss from time to time.

I wonder if I shall be a bit jealous of the old lady, Hanele thought to herself.

The room was large, furnished mostly in the period when Ivo's mother had married, and much of it reminded Hanele pleasantly of Polana in Grandfather's day. She took good care not to be caught out again looking round inquisitively, but she could not help noticing a portrait of a young man with a large nose, obviously Ivo's father, the old-fashioned armchairs, and the table laid with a white cloth for dinner. Then her eyes, wandering discreetly about the room, fell on something that gave her a pleasant surprise, *Mezzuzah**! There on the right doorpost, painted white like the wood, hung the *mezzuzah*, that dear, friendly little box with the scroll of parchment inside, that no Jewish door may be without!

'Are you looking at the *mezzuzah*, my dear?' asked the clever old lady, and Hanele blushed again. 'I'm afraid it's empty, though, the covenant of the Lord is no longer inside. We had the painters in, once, and we took the scroll out. Then they stopped the hole up with oil paint and we couldn't get it back. We forgot all about it and now I don't even know where it is. We are forgetting many things . . . And we no longer believe that the dear God loves us better than others, either.'

The old lady was looking at the girl with motherly eyes, examining her unobtrusively but carefully, not overlooking a single movement or glance. The girl appealed to her.

'Well, what shall we talk about, young lady?'

'Whatever you wish, ma'am, as long as I can understand it,' Hanele replied, and had a hard job to keep her voice natural.

'I know you are a clever girl. Later on you shall tell me something about yourself. Perhaps for the moment you would not mind talking about my son?'

'Of course, not . . .' Hanele whispered.

Ivo Karajich laughed out loud and kissed his mother's hand.

'Don't keep bothering me, Izzie,' said his mother and went on in her kind voice. 'I very much fear I shall not have the opportunity of meeting your parents, or at any rate, not for a very long time, and so you must forgive me, Hanichka, if I talk about something very unpleasant right at the start. I suppose you know that my son is not rich?'

Yes, Hanele knew that. That is to say, she knew Ivo was not rich according to Ostrava standards. Ivo's mother had obviously never seen Polana! Hanele thought of the magnificent shopping expedition in Prague. Why did the old lady keep on making her blush?

'I never for a moment doubted that he had told you. He studied at a business school, although I know there was something else that would have been far more attractive to him,' she nodded towards the bookcase. 'It just was not possible, then. They say he is good at his job, though, and he earns a good living. Looking back at the life the two of us were leading not so very long ago, I should say he was doing very well indeed.' Ivo was lolling across the sofa, his mother's hand held to his lips, and gazing at the ceiling. 'There would be no need to worry on that score.'

She gave the girl a searching look.

'There is something else to be given careful consideration, though. I said deliberately that I thought you were a clever girl. My son has told me you discovered very soon that he is mad.' Ivo gave a boisterous laugh.

'Unfortunately it's true, and it is a great misfortune. I really mean that, my child. I am sure you have heard how the Jews frequently accept baptism in these parts; we regard it with greater indulgence than you in the east, and we are used to it. You may also have heard that an Isaac Cohen may change his name to Ignatius Kolben or Joseph Kastner or any other ordinary-sounding name; Lord bless him, why shouldn't he, if he wants to – let him call himself George Kopecky if he likes. Now tell me whether you have ever heard of an Isaac Cohen who changes his name – here in Moravia, mind you – to Ivo Karajich? Isn't it terrible? I don't know what it's like at baptism, but I don't think it can be very pleasant. That was not enough for my son, though. He left the Catholic church and became a free thinker. Now you have this man, with that nose of his, getting up demonstrations against the bishop and preaching at funerals in the crematorium. And he really enjoys being called a stinking Jew at least once a week in the Catholic press, and being called a traitor and a renegade by the Zionists. He probably takes after his paternal grandfather, who calculated with absolute certainty every year that the Messiah would be bound to appear the following Easter, and that he had simply made a mistake in his calculations the year before. Now Izzie has taken it into his head to marry a girl from an orthodox Jewish family. If it meant he was returning to the fold – well and good. But it is not that. To anyone who does not know my son it just seems incomprehensibly illogical. If you want to get away from Jewry, then go as far away as possible – that is what anyone would think – am I not right? Last

117

week he started talking some nonsense about pure accident and other foolish things. But I can tell you what it is, my child, although he will never admit it: it is his blood calling him. In spite of all his funeral orations and all his anti-Jewish talk. I want to be just to him, even if he is my son. He is the kindest, most attentive and most charming son a mother could have, and you will not find a better husband anywhere in the world. You will have him. He is incredibly obstinate and always gets his own way. Perhaps that is because he was fatherless and I loved him unwisely. I do not want to hurt your feelings, Hanichka, but you must forgive an old woman: I think this marriage is sheer madness. As far as I am concerned, I shall give him my approval, just as I have always approved of whatever he does, and I think I shall be happy about it, too, but I am afraid he is not conscientious enough to realise clearly for himself the situation into which he is driving you. You surely cannot believe he is going to return to orthodox religion, and I do not think he would have tried to mislead you into thinking so. Are you prepared to give up the Jewish religion? What will your parents have to say about it? What will Polana have to say? Answer me, my child.'

'Now, mother . . .' Ivo began.

'Be quiet, Izzie,' she interrupted him. 'Let Hanichka answer for herself.'

While the old lady was talking Hanele had felt a chill come over her, followed by a fever, more than once, and now she was red in the face as she looked Ivo's mother straight in the eye, resolutely.

'We talked a great deal about it when we were in Prague. Do you think ma'am, that Ivo will not give way even when he sees he is making us both suffer?'

'I am afraid he won't, my child.'

'Then I shall give in. I would do anything in the world for him.'

'What about your family?'

Hanele gazed full into the ageing dark eyes which seemed so full of wisdom at that moment. She said slowly: 'It may be even worse than we think.'

The old eyes brightened. Now they were shining with a clear, calm light. 'I like the way you look at things, child.'

The old lady got slowly to her feet. 'It's time to have dinner. Come to the table, children, and let us talk about less serious things. I think my cakes turned out well today.' Standing, she kissed Hanele's forehead and went out.

Left alone together the two looked into each other's eyes and held hands for a moment. Hanele hurried after the old lady.

'Yes, that's right,' Ivo called after her, 'give Mother a hand.'

During dinner Ivo was back to his old ways. He kept making jokes and doing conjuring tricks with his knife and fork, calling the dill sauce spill sauce. He stroked his mother's hand and Hanele's in turn, and the old lady watched him with her clever eyes which smiled at him indulgently.

'There are times when I think I am a bad mother,' she said as she poured the coffee. 'Izzie drinks too much black coffee and he won't have it weak. I shall be glad if you break him of the habit.'

Then, as they talked and the old lady took no part in their conversation, Hanele saw she was looking from Ivo to her and back from her to Ivo, watching their faces and their gestures, and then gazing far beyond them. Her glance stopped at Hanele's eyes and stayed there even when Hanele looked up.

'You have very beautiful eyes, my child,' said the old lady. 'They are rather sad. Our poets call it the sorrow of thousands of years. I am afraid your eyes will become even sadder. Do you know what the eyes of the first generation look like? I mean the first generation to leave the Jewish faith and way of life. The people who throw all the ugly and beautiful fairy-tales on the rubbish heap, which is not where they belong, or else tidy the beautiful candlesticks and *talliths* and embroidered covers away in glass cases, which is where they really do belong. I have always found their eyes moving. There is much more than the sorrow of thousands of years in them. There is an uneasiness, a strange bitterness, an eternal anxiety, perhaps the fear of hurting those we have left, or those who have not yet accepted us as one of themselves. I am afraid your eyes will be like that, my daughter. And those of your children, perhaps, too . . . It cannot be helped . . . It cannot be helped, my child! . . . Do have another cake, Hanele, I think they were a success today,' she pressed food on Hanele, who had turned pale, and as she kept her eyes on the girl she took out a lace handkerchief and touched the corners of her eyes as though she had found a speck of dust there.

'Tralala, trala la,' Ivo sang noisily, 'you haven't seen anything yet, altogether, nothing at all, as our poet Slavomír Jaroboj Pšenička would say, that wasn't anything. Look this way, ladies and gentlemen! In one corner of this napkin, which, as you may see for yourselves, is quite empty, I place this little salt-cellar . . .'

'Izzie . . . oh, dear, Ivo, stop playing about,' Hanele was struggling between laughter and tears.

The old lady drew herself up and fixed her clever eyes on Hanele. 'What was that you said, my daughter? . . .' Her lovely mouth, so like that of her son, broadened in a smile. 'Did I hear you properly?'

Ivo was laughing his head off.

'Didn't you call him Izzie? . . .' the old lady gave Hanele a mischievous glance. 'Surely you didn't . . .?' And she gave a sideways glance at her son.

They all laughed. Hanele, happy to be able to relieve the tension within her, and catching Ivo's giggling fit, began to laugh in little broken gusts. The old lady was laughing out loud, too. Her teeth were still beautiful.

They carried on sitting together for a while, but did not return to the dangerous conversational ground.

After they had said good-bye and Ivo Karajich was going downstairs with his arm round Hanele's waist, he said: 'I am so happy, Hanichka.'

Preparations began that very week, gradually, as Ivo Karajich and Hanele wanted to set out the following Tuesday. It was actually a business trip through east Moravia, Slovakia and the western part of Sub-Carpathian Ruthenia, but Ivo wanted to take in Polana as well.

121

The winter weather was favourable, the roads were in a good state, there had not been too much snow, and the trip was practicable.

Hanele wrote to her parents. No, she did not tell them everything, she had not enough courage for that, but she said that at the end of the month or the beginning of the following month they would be coming to Polana. No reply came, indeed perhaps none should have been expected, for it is a long way to Polana and people there do not reply quickly.

By the hand of Mr Pšenička she sent Mr Ivo Karajich three letters of resignation: to the board of directors of the Cremation Society, the Secretariat of Free Thinking, and the editorial board of *The Free Thinker.*

And so one day a little yellow car hooted in front of Hanele's window, the car belonging to the firm of Dub & Arnstein, wholesale enamelware dealers, with seats for two and a big box for samples at the back. Hanele brought her things down and got in, the car drove through the streets, hooting a greeting to an old lady who waved from an upper window; a hand and a scarf waved from the car window, and it sped through Ostrava.

There was a heavy frost and Polana lay beneath a blanket of snow. The village was deserted; a ragged child, Jewish or Ruthenian, ran from one cottage to another to borrow some hot coals on a shovel, running as fast as it could over the snow to get back to the warmth. There were crows flying above the Shafars' farmyard and apple trees.

Pinches Yakubovich stood praying by a window that could not have been more than a foot across, facing east and looking on to the ash tree in the yard; his black and white striped *tallith* was about his shoulders, one square *tefillin** bound to his brow and the straps of the other twisted seven times round his bare left arm, through which the blood comes direct from the heart. Brana had gone into the village to get some hay for the cow, by borrowing, begging, weeping, shouting or threatening, because they had none left. The children kept creaking open the door to the yard, letting in the cold. Pinches Yakubovich was at his morning prayers: 'The Lord be praised and glorified, for He liveth. He liveth and the time of His being hath no end. He is the only God and there is none that is like unto Him in this uniqueness. He hath no bodily form nor is He a body, and there is nought to which His holiness may be compared.' When he came to the words: 'Behold, the Lord of creation reveals His majesty and His kingdom to all creation; the rich gift of prophecy hath He given to the man of His choice and glory,' Pinches Yakubovich wept. The big tears that ran down his sunken cheeks and fell on his *tallith* were tears of joy. This day, the greatest day in his life, the Lord God had called him by name: *lamet vav*.

Last night, before Tuesday came, Pinches Yakubovich had risen and put on his shroud to utter the terrible cabbalistic prayer *Khurban bayit*. When he came back from the ice-cold hallway with sweaty brow and frozen feet, into his warm bed, he had hardly fallen asleep when the angel of dreams had appeared to him.

'Arise, *lamet vav* Pinches!'

123

It had given him a fright and he had leapt out of bed to stand before the angel. He felt very ashamed to be standing there in torn pants.

'The Lord our God hath sent me,' the angel went on.

Pinches had no idea how the angel had got in, whether by the door or not. He was a tall young man in white robes and golden sandals, and as he sat on a chair by the table his head touched the beams of the ceiling. The natural position for his long legs would have been pointing in the direction of Brana's couch, with the stuffing coming out of it, but because he naturally did not want to risk touching it, at that particular time unclean, and because his feet were obviously cold, he had stretched them out towards the stove, so that he was sitting half turned away from Pinches.

The angel had spoken. At first in a dignified manner, although a seated angel warming his feet at the stove and talking over his shoulder does not look particularly dignified. As he went on, though, how careless and frivolous his tone had become! Clearly these were his words and not the Lord's own. Pinches had thought about it for the rest of the night. And he would go on meditating on it for a long time yet, if God so grant, for a hundred years.

'Thus speaketh the Lord unto you, in my words, *lamet vav* Pinches, son of Yankel! Your cries have reached Me and not passed unheard. I thought to break the Jewish congregation of Polana with an iron rod for their sins, like a potter's vessel, and scatter it like the sands of the desert. My wrath and anger have been turned aside by thy prayers, and I have taken pity upon them.

Behold, there are no *halutz* and no *mizrakhi* wrongdoers any more; I have swept them from the face of the earth as a thing unclean, and Polana will be one again as of old. But I demand a peace offering on behalf of the whole congregation. Only one, yet more terrible than any other. Death! Death! Death! Such a death as Polana has never seen, more terrible than the armed man, than fire or the grave, the death of all deaths. Tomorrow. Make this sacrifice without reluctance! That is one thing, *lamet vav* Pinches, son of Yankel. And then another thing: I can ignore the others, but not you. For heaven's sake stop bothering me about the Messiah! Who could put up with your annoying prayers and blasphemy and threats twice a week? I know best what I intend to do with My Jews and when to send Him. Then there'll be no need for your feet to get frozen, nor My angel. And the third thing: if you think I am going to turn Brana into a fish you are very much mistaken. She will partake with you of the glory of Heaven. That shows how little you understand My ways. Why did I create Brana? That in the sweat of her brow she might earn thy bread. There are limits to everything, don't forget. Get back to your tailoring! Solomon Fuchs is fast wearing out the seat of his trousers – ask him for the job! And that you, a tailor, should stand here in front of My messenger, shuffling your feet in pants as torn as those you've got on – shame on you!'

Standing by the window that looks on to the rim-covered trunk of the ash-tree, Pinches finished his morning prayers. He tidied away his *tallith, tefillin* and prayer-book under the bed in an old soap box. In his heart he could still hear the angel's words. And in his ears the double echo of the two themes of the message, as if the sound was coming from the far distance whence the angel had flown. Two themes mingling and interweaving, cutting one across the other, one of them a joyful Sabbath theme of '*Lamet vav!*' and the other the grim, sad theme of death, as if it were a lament in the half-light of the synagogue on the day of mourning. The grim melody of death was getting the upper hand over the bell-like melody of rejoicing, pushing it further and further away, then all of a sudden the gates of Heaven opened just a crack, the merry song disappeared inside, the gates of Heaven closed again, and on the earth there remained only the dark, terrifying melody: Death, death, death!

The very next day? In Polana?

Over his torn coat Pinches Yakubovich put on another shorter torn coat, and went out into the frost.

To whom in Polana would death come, more terrible than the armed man, the fire or the grave, such a death as Polana had never seen?

Pinches Yakubovich was meditating on horrible catastrophes, on crimes the like of which had never been heard, on torture, on desecrated corpses, on limbs torn apart and flung to the dogs and the swine. All that was not enough; it did not fit in with the prophecy. And so he thought of terrible demons and gathered together what history knows of their deeds.

He went to look around the village to see whether he could not find some sign of their early approach. He walked along with his head hunched between his shoulders, freezing in the cold, his hands thrust deep in his trouser pockets, and past the Shafars' house. There, in the tap-room, Joseph Shafar was breathing on the frozen panel of glass in the door and making a peep-hole through which to look out into the street. He saw Pinches Yakubovich. He tapped on the window, opened the door a crack, and called out: 'Hey, Pinches, come here a minute, will you?'

Is death to come to the Shafars? the thought came to the mind of the *lamet vav*.

Pinches obediently went across.

'Look here, Pinches,' said Joseph Shafar when they were both inside the house. 'You've travelled about a bit. Have you ever heard the name Karajich?'

'Karajich? No, I haven't. It might be a Turk, or something.'

'Couldn't it be a Jew?'

'No, not a Jew.'

For a whole fortnight Joseph Shafar had been carrying this name round in his head. Karajich! Karajich! Karajich! He had repeated it so often that he was no longer sure what it sounded like, and his wife kept confusing him by saying 'Of course it is!' and 'Wait and you'll see I'm right!' Of the firm of Dub & Arnstein: that would be right, of course. Commercial traveller: that would fit the case, too. But then: Karajich? Ivo? He had been intending to write to Hanele this past fortnight, but he had neither paper nor envelopes at home, and he could not send anyone to the Fuchses' for some because Solomon would know at once who it was for. Karajich. He could not sleep for thinking about the name, it worried him so. How cruel Fate can be! Yet there was nothing to be done, nothing at all, except to go on worrying and wait, perhaps another week, until they got here.

'Did you ever hear of a Jew named Ivo?'

'No, I never did.'

'Can a Jew have a name like that?'

'No, he cannot,' replied Pinches.

By this time the two lovers were no longer far from Polana, and already in country Hanele knew well. They had stopped in Hrihorovo, a village about halfway between Polana and the railway line, to feed and water the horses.

In the ten days of their journey they had driven right through Slovakia, speeding along roads where the snow lay dusting the roadside, and leaving behind them crucifixes at the crossroads where the cottage garden flowers at the feet of Christ had long since turned to bundles of frozen brown straw. They made frequent stops in towns and townships, and while Ivo called on his clients, Hanele waited for him impatiently, going over old manor houses, looking into the shop windows in the town squares, and peeping inquisitively into the little Jewish shops. They slept in hotels and in village inns which had nothing in common with that room in Prague except the scented sweetness of the nights and the satin lamp-shades on the bedside tables. It had been a journey of beautiful sights, sound health and great tenderness.

Then one afternoon they drove across a bridge, over the railway line, past the station and into the streets of

Hanele's district town, with the shops she knew and the hotel porter who seemed familiar, and as Hanele climbed out of the car with a rather cramped chest she suddenly felt the trip through Slovakia was far, far behind them. Beyond the plain there were snow-topped mountains visible on the horizon.

'Can we get to Polana from here?' Ivo Karajich asked the waiter who was standing by the hotel window watching the snow falling outside.

'By car, sir?' the man smiled. 'You'll be lucky to get through on a sledge.'

They hired a sledge from a Ruthenian farmer, Dvujlo. They also borrowed from him piles of furs edged with woollen fringes that looked like fleece. Ivo bought felt boots to slip on over his own. The journey before them would last at least ten hours, and perhaps twelve if they stopped to rest.

At half-past three in the morning the sledge was ready for them in front of the hotel; the oil torch stuck on the sledge frame by the nearest horse threw a fitful light on a stretch of the deserted street and the fresh snow that had fallen in the night. The frost pinched their nostrils in. They wrapped the furs well around themselves and got into the sledge, wriggling about in the hay to make as comfortable a hollow for each body as they could. Then they set out into the night, bells tinkling.

Now they were at Hrihorovo, feeding the horses. In a Jewish posting inn. Ivo laid Hanele down to sleep, wrapped up in furs, on an old oil-cloth couch in an icy parlour where there was nothing but a table, a couple of crates, and cobwebs in the corner. She slept. Ivo Karajich sat in the empty bar with the owner of the sledge, Andrij Dvujlo, drinking a brown liquid given the name of tea. With a smile, but nevertheless speaking in monosyllables, he refused to answer the questions showered on him by the inn-keeper's wife in her reddish wig: where had the gentleman come from? Had the gentleman come on business? Was the gentleman travelling in the company of Hanele Shafar of Polana? Then he went out to the farmyard to see the horses standing there with blankets over their backs, hoar frost forming around their mouths, and tufts of hay falling on the snow beneath them.

It was a long time since he had felt so well and refreshed. What a wonderful journey – across the white plain with mountains ahead of them and mountains behind them, with the sun breaking so suddenly through the morning sky and gleaming on the plain until its reflections were dazzling to the eye, with the thundering of the horses' hooves in the frost, with the bells keeping time to the thudding, and with their lovers' hands seeking each other with some difficulty under the piles of wraps and the clothes they were muffled in, and seeking their bodily warmth. Now he was delighted, looking at the walls of undressed timber and the only table the miserable inn possessed, at the bewigged woman piling long beech logs into the stove, and looking through the window at the Ruthenian women hurrying through the snow in their sheepskin coats, at a bearded Jew in tall felt boots who came out in front of his shop across the way, rubbed his hands and disappeared inside again. As he breathed the unusual atmosphere he smiled, repeat-

ing to himself over and over again: 'Gogol, Book One.'
He was not thinking of the fact that they were now only
five hours' journey away from Polana.

He went softly into the parlour to peep at Hanele. She
was red-cheeked from the biting frost, and was sleeping
calmly.

How beautiful she is, he thought . . . Had the world
ever seen such a wonderful mouth? . . . What luck for
me, finding you, my little one!

Then, after peeping at her five or six times, he came
and stood before her, stood to attention, clicked his heels
in military fashion and reported: 'My honoured and
noble mistress, the samovar is prepared. The horses are
waiting, Your *Prevoskhodityelstvo.*'*

Together with the farmer, Andrij Dvujlo, they sat
down in the inn to eat scrambled eggs and *barkhes* left
over from Friday and now rather stale, and to drink tea.

The inn-keeper's wife tried to start a conversation
with Hanele and asked her something in Yiddish.
Hanele replied rather unwillingly, and Ivo Karajich,
although he had not understood a word, answered her
with a smile in spite of the malicious imitation of her
intonation with which he spoke: 'That's right, my name
is Ivo Karajich, I come from Ostrava. I am thirty-three,
I travel for the firm of enamelware wholesale Dub &
Arnstein, I am extremely rich and I am on my way to
Polana to ask for the hand of Hanele Shafar in marriage.'

The woman gave a hurt smile.

Before they got back into the sledge and found the
seats they had hollowed out for themselves in the hay,

Ivo Karajich nervously felt in his breast pocket for his notecase.

Hanele noticed the movement and a pang of anxiety held her breath for a moment. In that notecase was Hanele's birth certificate, the document that proved she had come of age a mere three weeks ago.

The horses were rested and flew along the frozen road, the plain grew narrower and they drove into the mountain corridor, soon so narrow that there was only room for the road and the little stream, frozen almost right across.

Once more he felt for her hand among their fur wraps, but it lay there motionless.

In winter the sun sinks behind the mountains around Polana soon after three, and it was twilight before they got there.

When they reached a house on the edge of the village, Hanele spoke: 'Tell him to stop here, Ivo. Burkal has got room for the horses and we haven't – there's wood stored in the stable. I don't want people looking out to see who it is, either. They always know a stranger's sleigh-bells. It's only twenty minutes' walk from here.' Her breath was coming harder again.

They threw off the piled-up furs and got out. Hanele turned her coat collar up. They were passing the first of the cottages.

'You were enjoying the journey so much,' she said after a while, 'and I didn't want to spoil it for you. I waited until we had got this far. I was thinking a lot about it all, last night. This is the way you want it, and this is the way it will be; I still don't quite understand why, but I have learned a few things during these three months. Perhaps your mother was right when she said there was no help for it. You are like them, they are like you; but neither of you will give in because you think that would be the end of the world. I am caught between the two of you, and I shall get the worst of it. I do not know what is going to happen. They may take me away, out of the house, and you won't see me again, here. There aren't many places where they can hide me. Perhaps in the Abrahamoviches' cottage, or the Kahans', I hardly think they'd take me to the *mikvah*. Away from Polana there's only my two sisters. Don't forget that I am the first to take such a step and that what I am doing has never been done before in Polana. I shall only resist as far as it's absolutely necessary. You will be able to find me easily, but don't look for me, you will only make things worse. The most important thing is not to panic. Let things take their own course. I'll find my way back to you – tomorrow, in a week, in a year, even if I have to come barefoot. I've got the money for the journey hidden safely away.'

They were passing the Fuchses' house. The frozen ground rang beneath their steps. Fine snow began to fall. 'In Ostrava I often wondered whether what we are doing now is not just a waste of time, since there is so little hope – in fact, none at all, and whether it wouldn't be better just to send a written announcement of our marriage. But I was wrong – it is better this way. I have to say good-bye. It's the proper thing, to arrange the funeral. I only hope it will not be a noisy one.'

133

They passed the Katz's yard in the darkness, and if Hanele, anticipating this moment, had ever thought her heart would beat faster, she was wrong. She did not even realise they were passing the place.

They were drawing near to the Shafar house, that great dilapidated place, standing out against the evening twilight and the falling snow. Grandfather's house!

She did not tell him this was it, not even when they stood in front of it. She simply stopped and pressed his hand urgently. 'My darling, don't desert me now!' There was nothing in her calm voice, it was only that endearment that betrayed how great her anxiety was. She was already running up the three millstones piled up instead of steps, to the balcony, and resolutely opening the door to the kitchen.

Ivo Karajich went after her. He saw nothing but darkness and the holes in the stove door glowing red in that darkness.

Hanele went up to a vague shadow in the room. 'It's me, Mother!' and she mingled with the shadow, obviously in an embrace.

'Father! Father!' her mother called out joyously.

'This is Mr Karajich,' said Hanele.

Her father appeared from somewhere. From the way he shook hands his embarrassment was obvious.

Mother took a spill and lit it at the stove, to light the oil lamp. Her hands were shaking so badly that Hanele had to do it for her. The yellow flame shining in the shadows of the dying day reminded her of that early morning, three months earlier, when she had driven away from here.

With the first light from the lamp both her parents turned their faces towards their guest. Her mother's eyes lit up and her smile was one of welcome.

Her father could not take his eyes off this suitor. Then his face gradually broadened. More and more. And even more. So did his mouth. And his eyes. Look at that! That great big nose, the like of which he had never seen in the whole of Ruthenia! Those lovely almond-shaped eyes beneath coal-black brows. Those well-cut lips! Those cheeks, as black after half-a-day's delay in shaving as the face of Nakhamkes's apprentice! A great weight fell from Joseph Shafar's heart, giant boulders rolled away, and after them a shower of stones, leaving the heart free, bare, warm, beating. Joseph Shafar was offering his heart to Ivo Karajich on outstretched palms.

'Welcome, welcome!' he grasped his guest's hand in both of his own, and his face was smiling. 'You are very welcome, very welcome indeed, Mr Karajich.' The terrible name that had caused him so much anxiety suddenly seemed familiar and pleasant. Pinches was a fool! He was a fool, too! What a wise woman his wife was. He turned to her happily, and they smiled at each other, full of understanding.

Then he went over to Hanele again, as though he had not already welcomed her once. 'Welcome home, Hanele, welcome home, daughter!'

'I haven't got a thing for your supper!' Mother exclaimed suddenly in a despairing voice.

Ivo Karajich asked Hanele to show him over the house she had told him so much about, before it got too dark. And feeling intuitively that neither he nor she would ever again have the chance to enjoy the place that had sheltered her childhood, Hanele showed him the deserted tap-room and shop (although her father protested), took him through the half-empty rooms where the loose boards rocked, took him to look at the farmyard where the poultry tracks were now covered in snow, the sheds and the farm buildings. She did not take him into the orchard, though, as her memories of that spot were too unpleasant.

It really felt like a leave-taking, when everything seems to come to life in a strange manner, and we caress and want to stroke things if not with our hands, at least by a fond glance. Father, who had his own explanation for this general survey of the place, and accompanied them a little uneasily, kept on smiling and doing his best to be pleasant. He felt the constant need to touch his son-in-law's sleeve, thinking in vain of what he could boast about; he talked about the glory of Grandfather's times. Every now and again Hanele was called into the kitchen to answer her mother's questions, which she did in a cursory, unwilling fashion – oh, what did it matter, Mother? she thought to herself! – Was he rich? Wouldn't he want a dowry? Was he kind? Did he come from a good family? Were his parents still alive? Then she ran back to the snow falling lightly on the farmyard, to be able to press her lover's arm in the darkness, or to be able to say in a matter-of-fact voice, as though she was explaining something to him as she scratched Bryndusha between her horns and laid her head fondly on the animal's neck: 'I adore you, my darling.' Or, as she closed the barn-door and latched it: 'Have you observed, my darling, that I adore you?' And he realised that she was speaking in such bookish phrases in front of her father because Joseph Shafar's understanding of Czech was not so good.

Then they had supper in Grandfather's old room which led off the tap-room. Tea, scrambled eggs, and a bit of *barkhes* left over from the Sabbath and somewhat stale; her mother was upset that she had nothing better to offer this guest, for whom she had been waiting for years in constant fear that he might never come. Hanele was absent-minded and increasingly uneasy. Ivo Karajich, on the other hand, was optimistic, talking happily about Ostrava and their journey across Slovakia; he made jokes and Mother was happier than ever about him. Father, though, in spite of his happy smile, was not listening with all his mind; he guessed that there was an unpleasant interview ahead of him that very day, perhaps very soon. He was only mistaken about its subject.

Hanele could not bear the tension any longer. She could not stand it. Let it be decided now, at once! As they finished their tea and her mother got up to fetch more, she rose too, saying: 'Come along, Mother, Ivo and Father have got to have a talk.'

She turned pale. She looked at Ivo. Her mother was looking at him beseechingly, too. They went out of the room.

Ivo Karajich lit a cigarette. He was smiling faintly. Of course they would come to terms. Naturally! This was Europe, after all.

'I think Hanele wrote and told you that I love her, Mr Shafar, and that I should like to have your approval for our marriage. Before I ask for her hand, though, I should like to make several things clear; one thing, especially, I should like to explain.'

Joseph Shafar's heart was in a gentle whirl. 'My dear sir,' he replied, and his voice trembled with anxiety, 'I do not know whether Hanele has told you about our great misfortune. I gave my other daughters a large dowry. In the present state of things I cannot give Hanele much, but she is the only daughter I have left and everything I possess or may one day possess . . .'

'I know Hanele has no dowry, Mr Shafar. I do not ask for her dowry, I do not need it. I earn enough to keep a family decently. You need not worry about that.'

What a man! Karajich! Karajich! Karajich! What a wonderful man! Joseph Shafar's heart was rejoicing. The last weight that remained had fallen from it. What a wonderful day! Who could have hoped that such a day would ever come?

'You must love my daughter very deeply.'

Joseph Shafar's face was full of rejoicing too. Face to face with such happiness Ivo Karajich felt his courage fail, and he hesitated. 'Naturally I love your daughter very deeply,' he spoke to the glowing eyes and smiling mouth, 'or else I should not have come here to ask for her hand in marriage.' They were sitting facing each other. Between them, the white cloth and the tea-cups. Ivo Karajich nervously tapped the ash off his cigarette into one of the saucers. It has got to be, he said to himself. They were bound to reach agreement, surely! He spoke: 'I am thinking of something else, Mr Shafar, something I consider trifling, but you may have other ideas. Hanele tells me that we shall not agree, but I do not believe that. We must reach an understanding, and I am sure we shall. I am not a Jew, Mr Shafar.'

The older man's eyes bulged. 'I do not understand you, my dear sir,' he said in a whisper.

'I am not a Jew, Mr Shafar.'

The colour slowly drained from the old man's face. The glow left his eyes. Slowly his two hands gripped the edge of the table. Gradually he got to his feet. He stood there, leaning his weight on his palms, flat on the table, swaying forwards and backwards, his dead eyes fixed on nothingness, seeing nothing. He said again, as Hanele had done that day in Prague, 'You . . . you are not a Jew?'

'No, I am not.'

'You have been baptised?' The voice sounded strangled.

'I belong to no faith.'

'I beg your pardon; I do not understand Czech perfectly. Do you mean that you do not believe in the One God?'

'That is so.'

'That is even worse, sir.'

Now Joseph Shafar sat down again as slowly as he had risen to his feet. He seized his head in his hands. The blow which had cast him from the heights had been too sudden. His lifeblood seemed to be draining away and he wished only for death.

'Then what do you want here, sir?' he whispered.

Of what value, here, were all the stunning proofs he used at hundreds of lectures, meetings and public debates? And which of them would be at least valid enough for the old man to listen to with understanding? The one about God being a fiction of the imperfect human mind, which is not capable of understanding the essential nature of time and space and helps itself out by replacing one riddle with another? Or the one about social evolution, about the east, where simple conditions may still allow God validity and perhaps even justification, while in the west God has died and been replaced by new idols? Or would scientific proof be more suitable here, a lecture on the selection of species? Or a historical talk on the origin of the Bible and of a myth, the creation of Jehovah from the gods of Assyria, Babylon and Egypt, and all the changes He passed through in the course of history? Or should he use primitive arguments and absurd questions such as: who made God? Where did Cain's wife come from? How could Noah take a may-bug into the ark if it was autumn, and how could he take a gossamer-spider if it was spring? Or would the best approach be to appeal to paternal affection and beg him not to destroy two people's happiness for the sake of an idea, for a mere nothing, for smoke and haze? Or should he have recourse to mean subterfuge: the village will never learn that I am not a Jew, nobody will ever find it out?

Oh, no, Ivo Karajich could not even remember all the arguments he had used as Joseph Shafar sat there with sightless dead eyes, his temples in his hands and his fingers digging into the sparse grey hair on his head.

Was he listening? Did he hear at all? Had he let down the veils of his eyelids and stopped his ears with the soft lobes?

The old man's head sank lower and lower, until his forehead rested on the tablecloth. Then he raised his head as though ashamed of his weakness, straightened his shoulders and made an effort to speak: 'You will excuse me, sir; I shall be back in a moment.'

He went through the tap-room into the kitchen, where Dvujlo the peasant was having supper. He went on into the parlour. There was only a candle burning on the table.

Hanele was standing at the window, her head leaning back against the frame and her eyes staring motionless at the angle of the ceiling with the opposite wall. Her mother sat at the table in tears. It was clear that everything had been said here, too. Her father began walking agitatedly from one corner of the room to another, at every second step lifting his hand and letting it fall on his thigh with a slapping sound. He said not a word. He ran about the room like this for a while and then dashed out again.

Ivo Karajich was waiting for him in Grandfather's room. What nonsense it all was, he thought. He went forward to meet the other man.

'Mr Shafar,' he held out his hands towards the older man. 'Mr Shafar . . . over a trifle . . . Let me have Hanele! . . . You will never regret it . . .'

The old man sat down, this time on the chair next to Ivo Karajich, where the girl had sat. He looked him straight in the eye. The expression on his face was infinitely sad. 'Listen to me, my dear sir,' he said. 'You say you are not a Jew. You are wrong. Your parents, may the Lord grant them peace, were Jews. My dear sir, you are a Jew too. Whether you like it or not. You are still a Jew, even if you blaspheme and do not believe in God, and no societies and no baptism can take Jewry from you. You ought to be thankful that it is so, that you remain a royal prince with all his privileges, such as no one else has either in this world nor the next. But you do not believe in God . . . Listen, my dear sir! You have offered a glass of pure spring water to one suffering from thirst, and as he stretched out his hand longingly towards it, you have dashed it from his lips and broken it. Return to Israel! Do you know what it would mean for us, if our child were to marry a man who has forsaken God? Hanele has perhaps told you of the misfortunes that have attended us all our life. Blow after blow, and a hundred times have I longed to be dead. Yet what would that suffering be, compared to what you and my daughter would like to bring upon us? I should be worse than the leper, cast out from society. I should be deader than the dead. For what horror it is, to be dead and yet to walk among men! . . . Return to Israel, my dear, dear sir. Then I will give you my daughter, with all my heart I will give her to you, I will call down upon you the greatest blessings there are, I will love you, I will be the happiest man in Polana, I will rejoice and be glad for I shall have triumphed over my enemies . . . Oh, if only you knew what it would mean for me!'

Ivo Karajich thought over his words. He felt pity for the old man. 'I find it difficult to understand you,' he said. 'I don't see where the leper and the dead come into it, just because your daughter wants to marry an honest man. I do see, though, that it would be difficult for you to live here among these fanatics afterwards. Very well! I offer you a way out, and offer it with all my heart. Sell whatever you have and come and live with us in Ostrava. You will have the chance to work and we shall all benefit from it. Hanichka will be happier, too. I shall make you a good son-in-law and you will never regret it.'

Hanele's father shook his head gently. 'Thank you kindly, sir, but I shall not do that.'

Ivo Karajich frowned as he considered the matter. 'You said I had never ceased to be a Jew,' he remarked. 'What then do you mean by your "return to Israel"?'

'A formality, my dear sir,' and the old man reached his palms towards the younger man's face as though to beseech him and to caress him at the same time. 'Everything would be all right, then . . . ach, ach! everything would be all right, wonderful . . . wonderful, everything all right . . . all right, wonderful . . .'

Ivo Karajich saw the old man's eyes fill with tears. Ivo Karajich was moved. But he frowned. 'I was prepared for this suggestion, Mr Shafar, and I was afraid of it. I would do anything else for Hanele. This is the only thing I cannot do.'

The old man nodded his head slowly as if in agreement. 'Is that your last word?' he whispered.

'My last word on that point, Mr Shafar.'

The old man went on slowly nodding his head. Then he got to his feet and went out.

He was gone a long time. Five minutes came and went, over and over again. Ivo Karajich was waiting. A quarter of an hour passed. He frowned. He lit cigarettes and put them aside again, and the saucer was full of stubs. Then he too got up and began walking back and forth in the room. Why hadn't the old man come back? He looked at his watch. Half an hour? He was seized by fear for Hanele. He began to feel uneasy.

At last he heard Joseph Shafar in the tap-room. Ivo Karajich sat down again to wait for him to come in . . . Joseph Shafar did not appear . . . What was going on?

Ivo Karajich opened the door leading into the tap-room. A little candle was burning in the dark room. Hanele's father looked as though he was putting things straight on the counter. Only there was nothing there to put straight and it was clear he was only pretending. He did not turn round.

'Mr Shafar . . .'

He straightened up calmly. 'What can I do for you, sir?' He spoke politely, as if to a customer asking for a second glass.

Ivo Karajich took two steps forward. Through the open door from Grandfather's room the light and the smoke poured in. The room took on a strange colour and smell.

'Mr Shafar, I should like to speak to Hanele.'

'I am afraid that will not be possible. Hanele is asleep now.' His eyes were as cold as pebbles in the frost.

Ivo Karajich pulled out his watch. 'Now? It's only seven o'clock.'

'We go to bed early in the winter, sir.'

Ivo Karajich took a few quick steps towards the kitchen door and turned the knob. The door was locked. He turned around. The iron-plated door leading to the street was closed too. Was he a prisoner? Panic-stricken, he suddenly had vision of sinister rituals being enacted.

'Why is the door locked?' he cried.

'We always lock up at night, sir.'

'Where is Hanele? I want to speak to her.'

'She is asleep.'

Ivo Karajich banged on the kitchen door. 'Hanele!' he called. 'Hanele!'

There was no answer. He waited. Silence.

'Hanele!' he shouted at the top of his voice.

Joseph Shafar stood there calmly, looking straight in front of him. 'There is nobody there,' he said in a little while.

'You are lying! My driver is in there.'

'I am telling the truth, sir. Your driver has taken your boxes over to the Fuchses'.'

'What does this mean?' Ivo Karajich replied angrily. 'Are you refusing to put me up in a public inn?'

'I must ask you to forgive me. Our religion does not permit a man to sleep under the same roof as the girl he wishes to marry. At the Fuchses' you will have a clean room, far more comfortable than any I could offer you.'

'Where is Hanele?'

Joseph Shafar did not answer. Like an obstinate boy. As if he had not heard the question.

Ivo Karajich thought the matter over. What should he do? Should he pull his revolver out of his pocket and force the old man to speak? Should he pick up a chair and start banging at the door until he broke it down? Should he go out into the village and bang on the cottage windows and shout to the whole world that fanatical Jews were holding a girl prisoner and torturing her?

He was tormented with anxiety for her. Both head and heart were in turmoil. 'You have no right to keep her prisoner!' he exclaimed. 'You know she is of age, don't you?'

'You remind me of the fact, sir.'

He had made up his mind. He would search the whole village for her. 'Perhaps in the Abrahamoviches' cottage, or the Kahans', I hardly think they'd take me to the *mikvah,*' he could hear her saying.

'Open the door!' he shouted. He noticed his coat and hat lying ready on the table.

First he gathered all his strength and calmness together and went over to Joseph Shafar. 'Mr Shafar, perhaps we are both too worked up,' he said, trembling from head to foot. 'Perhaps we ought to postpone our discussion until tomorrow. But you must realise one thing: we shall not give each other up, she is of age, we belong to each other. I will find her. For God's sake, I want to settle this in a friendly way; let me have her!'

The old man shook his head slowly but resolutely.

'Then tell me where she is, at least!'

The old man shook his head again.

Wild fury and exasperation seized Ivo Karajich. 'Very well, then. You want force. You'll get it! I shall come and fetch her!'

He turned to leave. As he reached the door he turned back and said, hoping to hurt the old man: 'I forgot. What do I owe you for my own and my fiancée's supper?'

The old man frowned. He half closed one eye and looked at the floor. Then he looked up at Ivo Karajich again and answered politely: 'Hanele still belongs to me, today, sir; you owe me nothing for her. For yourself it makes two crowns eighty hellers.'

Ivo Karajich laid the money down on the table and Joseph Shafar unlocked the door, locking it behind him.

Ivo Karajich did not go down the three millstones that led from the balcony to the street. With rapid strides he followed the balcony round three sides of the house.

'Hanele!' he shouted at the top of his voice.

Then he ran down into the farmyard. 'Hanele!'

There was no sound. The light in the inn went out.

Ivo Karajich ran through the dark night to the Fuchses'. Night had fallen in Polana.

He knew what to do: 'At the Kahans', at the Abra-hamoviches', hardly likely to be in the *mikvah*.' As he thought of the *mikvah* there passed through his mind not the words, but a sense of all the anti-Semitic tales of ritual crimes, and a breath as of lukewarm blood and water.

There was light at the Fuchses', both in the shop and the house. If Hanele thought they had passed through the darkening village unobserved, she was wrong. A few hours earlier, as they passed the Fuchses' house, Sura had been peeping out into the half-light of the street, peering around the advertisements hanging on

147

the glass doors. Was not that the figure and gait of Hannah Shafar? she thought to herself. Had Hannah Shafar run away from the *hakhshara*? Who was the man she had brought with her? How had they got here? Had they left a sleigh at the Burkals'? Sura Fuchs was terribly excited.

She put on her coat and went out into the snow that was falling lightly. Catching sight a moment later of a stranger carrying two suitcases, she asked him politely: 'Have you brought Hannah Shafar home?'

'Yes, I think that's the name. I'm just on my way there. Can you tell me where it is?'

'It's quite near. Who is the gentleman?'

'I couldn't say. He's a Czech.'

'They are going to get married?'

'Looks like it.'

Sura went back home, locked the shop door and went through to her mother and sisters in the parlour. 'News!' She was wearing her sweet-sour smile. 'Hannah Shafar has come home from Ostrava. She has brought a suitor with her. The suitcases are real leather.'

That evening they were astonished to see the man with the suitcases coming to their house. What was going on? She was burning with curiosity. She dragged Andrij Dvujlo into the kitchen.

Hadn't he made a mistake? Joseph Shafar had really sent him there? To their place, to the Fuchses'? The gentleman was coming along, too, in a little while? Was it really Shafar who had said so? Joseph Shafar, a tall man with a black beard going a bit grey? (She looked sideways at her mother and Esther shrugged her shoulders uncomprehending.) The gentleman was sitting in the little room with Mr Shafar and the girl with her mother in the parlour? What else? . . . What else? . . . But that was all Dvujlo had to tell.

Here was the gentleman himself. As Ivo Karajich opened the shop door and the bell tinkled as it shook on its coiled spring, Sura was on the spot in an instant, with a pleasant smile. Solomon and Esther Fuchs came in to greet the stranger, too. Sura's heart was thumping.

She took him into the best room, quite a citified one by Polana standards. 'Would you like supper, sir?'

'No, thank you,' he answered testily. 'Is the driver here?'

'He's in the kitchen.'

'Would you send him to me, please?'

Sura had a little laugh all to herself in the hall. The gentleman had come to seek his bride! The gentleman with a bad temper had come to the young lady's rival! It was as clear as daylight: they had not settled the bargain in old Abraham's little room. Hannah had told her suitor that her dowry was heaven only knows how big, and the young man had not let himself be caught and had run away just in time!

'They couldn't agree about the dowry at the Shafars',' she reported back to her father and sisters in the parlour, and went out to the kitchen to take the same news to her mother.

Ivo Karajich opened his suitcase and took out an electric torch. When Andrij Dvujlo came in he said: 'I shall need you all night. I will pay you twice as much as we agreed on.'

It was not easy to understand each other in two different languages but they managed it somehow.

'One more thing. Were you in the kitchen when Miss Shafar left? Do you know whether she went along the balcony towards the farmyard, or down into the street?'

'I didn't see her, but I'm sure she did not leave the house.'

'How do you know?'

'She wasn't dressed to go out and she hadn't even got boots on. She took them off in the kitchen soon after we got there.'

'Tell me everything!'

'Let me see, now, the Jewess went out somewhere, then she came back and in a little while another Jewess came in. I expect she had sent for her. The young lady went out with them.'

'Were they holding her?' A chill went down Ivo Karajich's spine.

'No.'

Was Hanele really still in the house, he wondered. That would mean changing his plans. Why had she not answered his shouts if she were there? Had the women taken her somewhere and gagged her? Hadn't he better call the police after all? 'The most important thing is: don't create a panic,' Hanele had said. He wouldn't, yet. Was there really anything going on? Wasn't it just that he was over-excited, imagining the sort of idiotic scene housemaids enjoyed in cheap novels?

'Have you served in the army, Dvujlo?'

'Yes, sir, I was a corporal.'

'Good. This is a serious matter, I don't want you to ask any questions; later on I'll tell you what it's all about. Go and put your things on, we shall be out of doors all night, watching the Shafars' house. Take on four men, will you, Ruthenians. No, you'd better make it six. Fix what we're going to pay – offer them plenty. You can tell them anything you like, but I don't want them asking me questions.'

'Don't create a panic!' . . . Was he behaving like a fool, he wondered? Mad, like his mother always said?

In the hall Dvujlo was putting on his sheepskin coat.

'Now where are you off to?' Sura poked her head out of the kitchen.

'Just to look round.'

She kept her eye on them, though, and when she saw the two of them go out together she ran excitedly into the room. 'Benjie!' she shouted at her brother, 'They're going out. Get your coat on quick and run after them.' Then she hurried into the best room to see whether the suitcases were still here. They were.

Dvujlo went round in the darkness knocking on cottage windows and waking people up; those who had just gone to sleep grumbled unwillingly as they put their heads out of tiny windows. Meanwhile, Ivo Karajich was trying to find his way around to the back of the Shafars' house, the way Etelka had escaped that day, long ago, with the soldiers after her. He wanted to make sure there were no tracks leading away from the house on that side, but he got tangled up in fences and hedges and fell into pits full of snow, and was glad when he managed to scramble back to the road in safety.

The men were soon gathered together. 'A witch hunt?' thought Dvujlo. 'We've seen that sort of thing before.'

Ivo Karajich sent one man to the Abrahamoviches', one to the Kahans' and one to the *mikvah* to see if they could see lights anywhere. Another led him over the stiles the Ruthenians had put up in the fences, so that cattle could not get over but a man could, and took him down to the stream. Flashing his torch over the snow Ivo Karajich satisfied himself that the deep snow that had lain for some time was untouched by tracks of man or beast. To be on the safe side, though, he put a man on guard on that side too.

When they got back to the road the men reported that two women had gone into the house.

'Who were they? Did you recognise them?'

'Faiga Kahan from the *mikvah* and Raisa Abrahamovich,' Ivan Moskal told him.

'Who are they?'

'Just Jewesses.'

Ivo Karajich got them to light a fire in one of the cottages, and light a lamp, so that four could rest and sleep while the other four were on watch. It was the first time he had been inside a Carpathian cottage, and its hard clay floor, the gloomy light of a stable lamp without its globe, the bread oven and the hollowed-out log cradle, which served as a hanging from the ceiling above the bed, seemed to him unreal and melodramatic. He set his men on guard, and with Mytra Datz hid himself behind the fence around Moskal's cottage, which was just across the road from the Shafars.

It had stopped snowing and the moon was coming through the clouds. He waited. Waiting is a slow business, at night, and the time between one cigarette and the other is shorter than we think it is.

What did he really expect to see except the white night, the piled-up castles of snow-clouds above his head, illuminated by the moon, or a bit of the street and the outlines of the Shafars' house? Or was he standing here, moving his weight from one foot to the other, just to look at two Jewish women going into a house? Or was his imagination hungering for a scene from some bloodthirsty melodrama, for mysterious sleighs and hooded figures climbing out of them, for an obscure bundle carried out of the house, its black cover making him suspect a girl's body gagged and bound? He was going mad!

But he did not wait in vain. About half an hour later the iron door in the dark house creaked open. In the darkness, the seconds between one sound and the next, which we expect to hear, are long, and unsettling. The door creaked shut. A man came down from the balcony; it had to be Joseph Shafar.

'Follow him!' Ivo Karajich whispered to Mytra Datz.

Then the men he had sent to reconnoitre came back and reported all dark at the Kahans', the Abrahamoviches' and the *mikvah*. They had met Faiga Kahan and Raisa Abrahamovich as they went. Ivo Karajich knew that already . . . It was strange how much was going on that night.

Before long three women came up to the house. They climbed up to the balcony and softly knocked on a shuttered window, a slight sound that penetrated the silence, and the house mysteriously swallowed them up.

'Who was that?' Ivo Karajich whispered.

'Miriam Herschkovich, Khava Gleizer, and the other may have been Rifka Eizigovich,' Ivan Magyarchuk answered him. 'They are all friends of Hanele Shafar.' What were they doing there?

When all was quiet again and the street deserted, Ivo Karajich came out of his hiding-place behind the fence and strode rapidly across the street. He climbed the three millstones to the balcony and went around the building on tiptoe, his fingers just touching the cold snow lying on the hand-rail. The loud creak of the boards beneath him scared him. He reached the back of the house, where the balcony ended, and where everything was as dead as elsewhere in the house, for the windows were shuttered fast and it was dark behind them . . . No! . . . From one of them, the last, a tiny crack of yellow light filtered through.

He crept up to it. There were no doors on this side of the house, and there was little danger of giving himself away. He tried to peep around the shutter barred on the outside. It could not be done, nor could he manage to widen the slit with his fingers or a knife. It was just broad enough to let a crack of light through, like a thin strip of paper, and it showed only a blank white wall.

He had to rely on his ears. He listened.

There was a conversation going on inside. They were clearly women's voices.

He could hear little and he could not guess the meaning or catch even a single word. The women seemed to be speaking Yiddish. Was not that Hanele's voice?

Then there was a pause . . . Then a few more words. As if the people inside had said all they wanted to say and had nothing more left to tell each other. Like relatives faced with the thankless task of comforting the mourning family before the funeral.

Yes, that was certainly Hanele's voice! She was answering a high-pitched soprano, perhaps one of her friends.

Quite as important for Ivo Karajich was what he did not hear, and the lack of it calmed him down. There were no shrieks of revenge, no cries of pain, no groans, nothing that gave any hint of violence.

Mad! it was his mother's voice in him . . . Acting in that extravagant way in an unfamiliar village . . . The housemaid reading her penny-dreadful in bed is wiser, she only believes it up to the last page, and when she's finished the book she wraps the bedclothes around her and goes to sleep . . . He, on the other hand, has to start playing at detectives!

A moment later he found himself in a really crazy situation. A board creaked on the balcony. Cautious steps could be heard. Now what? The balcony only ran around three sides of the house, and this was the third. Should he jump down into the orchard? He would only draw attention to himself by the noise he would be bound to make in falling. The only thing left for him to do was to crouch hurriedly in one corner, where the shadows were deepest.

It was a boy. He was walking on tiptoe, but with assurance, as though he felt at home. He came right up to Ivo Karajich and swung himself up on the hand-rail of the balcony. A handful of snow fell on Karajich's knees. Straight as a die the boy dropped from the rail on to the wall. Leaning his palms against the wall he squinted down through the gap above the shutters. He seemed to know his way about all right.

Ivo Karajich swore. He could see the funny side of his situation, the cautious way he crouched, swearing there in the silence, with a lump of cold snow on his knees and a boy with legs astride above him. He was laughing at himself. How long was that long-legged frog going to stand over him?

He stood there for a long time. At long last the boy crept away, listening carefully at the corner of the house in case there was anyone about. Ivo Karajich followed soon afterwards.

'A boy went into the house,' Ivan Magyarchuk reported from behind the fence. 'He's just come out. I couldn't say for certain, but I think it was Benjie Fuchs.'

Except for the name, Ivo Karajich already knew all that. The snow was falling heavily now, hiding the Shafars' house from sight; the street was soon deep in snow, the great flakes pilling up softly like down.

Joseph Shafar took his time coming back. An hour, an hour and a half. Meanwhile four women wrapped up in shawls left the house, unrecognisable in the snow-storm. That meant that one of the visitors had remained inside, and Ivan Magyarchuk was of the opinion that it might be Faiga Kahan, judging by the size of the four other figures.

At last! On the white road the figure of Joseph Shafar emerged from the whirling snowflakes. He was covered in snow, and put one foot before the other as if exhausted. The man with him, though, wrapped up to the eyes like a woman, in a long coat and scarves wrapped around his neck and over his cap and his ears, moved even more slowly.

'Who is that with him?' Ivo Karajich asked in a whisper.

'Old Mordecai.'

'Who's that?'

'Their Jewish holy man.'

Mordecai Yid Feinermann was indeed having great difficulty in getting along, and Joseph Shafar had to help him up the three millstone steps. They could hear them stamping on the balcony to rid their boots of clogging snow, and then the snow-covered house swallowed them up too. Strange how many visitors that house welcomed in the night!

The white darkness of the night persisted and as the guards went off duty they sought out the roaring log fire in Moskal's stove, took off their felt boots, dried their footrags, and lay down for two hours wherever they could find room in the little hovel crowded with men, women and children. The peasants knew what was afoot now. It was not spies the stranger was after. It was a girl. They laughed. 'Fancy him thinking the Jews would let him have her!' Their final opinion was in agreement with that of Ivo's mother. Ivo Karajich kept watch all night long. The stuffy heat and the fleas in Moskal's place were a bit too much for him. He paid out wages and handed around his cigarettes.

When daylight came, and it was unlikely that they would take Hanele away if they had not already done so under cover of darkness, he put the last men on guard and waded his way through the snow to the Fuchses', leaving the first tracks in the street. He did not want to go to sleep, but to warm himself and wash and shave. He dismissed the nagging hint of shame he felt for having started a panic in the village by telling himself that at least he now knew where Hanele was.

The Fuchses' house was still locked, but Sura answered his first knock and opened the door to him in her dressing-gown.

'You have been out all this time on a visit, sir?' she asked innocently. She knew the whole story by then. What a sensational business!

'A *goy*?' she said to herself as candle in hand she took Ivo Karajich to his room, observing his great nose with a sideways look. 'A nose like that on a *goy*?'

The Jews were troubled. They were amazed. They were hurt. They were horrified. They were furious.

What? . . . Ha–ne–le . . .? Ha-ne-le Shafar?

What? . . . A Jew who does not believe in God?

Let Baynish Zisovich, at the first opportunity, as soon as day breaks, harness his horse and ride straight away into the town, let him go at a gallop and not spare the horses! Let him bring the Rabbi straight back with him! And indeed, the whole community could see Zisovich's

Julie thundering wildly through the pale light of morning and see Baynish in his chariot like Judah in the valley of Ajalon, flourishing the reins and curling his whip over the horse's head.

There you are, you see! Was not Mordecai right – if you take away but an accent, all is destroyed? There you are, indeed. A tassel on the *tsitsith* has fallen to the ground, and this is the outcome!

Unhappy Joseph Shafar! Poor Mother! Then, remembering suddenly the real heart of the sin, they shouted horror-stricken: 'Do you realise that this is the first time any Jew has forsaken God since Polana has been Polana?' What will happen next? Oh Lord, what will happen next? What plagues hath the Lord not sent on Polana this year to punish it? First there was the desecration of the *mikvah*. Then the dreadful ideas of the Zionists, the *halutz* and *mizrakhi*. And now this! Can you not understand, can you not comprehend, can you not see in this the finger of God upraised in warning? Do not allow it! Do not suffer it! Do not let it happen!

The terrible news flew from mouth to mouth. It flew around the cottages even before the night was over. Women ran out thrusting bare feet into shoes and throwing shawls over naked shoulders, wading through the snow and knocking on other cottage windows to be let in. Have you heard the news? Sleepy people jumped out of bed in their shifts, oil lamps were lit in the low rooms, and long shadows crept across the walls. To the homes of Raisa Abrahamovich and the parents of Miriam, Khava and Rifka, who had seen the misfortune at first hand, came streams of visitors.

159

Next morning every man of any standing in the community turned up at Mordecai Yid Feinermann's. The wise old man sat nodding his head sorrowfully, and his three bearded sons nodded likewise; without bothering to answer unnecessary questions, the old man issued short commands from his bench by the stove.

No, Mordecai Yid Feinermann did not fail at the moment of greatest trouble. In all the fuss about the *halutz* and the *mizrakhi* followers he might use the veils of his eyelids and the stoppers of his earlobes to indicate his reaction, for that was a silly, trifling little thing that was not worthy even of a corner of his soul's attention, which belonged to the Lord; but now the time was grave, for Israel, the Lord and the honour of the community was at stake.

Is it true that all the respected Jews visited Mordecai Yid Feinermann that morning?

No, it is not.

'Has Pinches Yakubovich been here?' he asked.

'No.'

With the help of his sons the old man put on his outdoor clothes; one of them pulled on his high felt boots for him, the other wrapped scarves around his throat and ears, and he set out to walk into the village.

With his sons he stopped at Pinches Yakubovich's cottage. 'Do you know what has happened at the Shafars'?' he spoke wrathfully, hurt that Pinches had not thought to come to him himself.

'Yes, I know,' Pinches answered quietly.

'Come along then!' Mordecai Yid Feinermann said sternly.

At that moment a strange thing happened, something quite incomprehensible: Pinches Yakubovich, instead of reaching for his coat, stood there gazing into a corner and replied: 'I am not coming.'

The insult was even worse than Mordecai Yid Feinermann had thought. The old man went closer to him. Beneath his beetling white brows his eyes blazed more with amazement than with anger. 'It is possible that I have not understood you properly,' he said. 'Do you refuse your help in affliction, at the most terrible time in the life of our community?'

'I do refuse,' Pinches Yakubovich answered humbly.

The old man's eyes were aflame with the indignation of the Lord. He raised his fist. 'Woe unto you, Pinches!'

And his sons repeated: 'Woe unto you, Pinches! Do you call yourself a Jew? Shame on you!'

The old man went out. His sons turned once more and, not wishing to make a fuss at so serious a moment, contented themselves with looking Pinches up and down.

Yet Pinches Yakubovich could not act otherwise. A secret is a heavy burden to bear. Only the elect can bear it. The Lord's name be praised for the insult with which Mordecai Yid Feinermann had tried to humiliate him! The Lord his God had said to him through the mouth of His angel: 'I demand a peace-offering. One on behalf of the whole congregation. Tomorrow. Make this sacrifice without reluctance.' Could there be any doubt, after the news that Brana and the children had brought in from the street that morning, who was to be that sacrifice? 'Death! Death! Death! Such a death as Polana has never seen, more terrible than the armed man, than fire or the grave, the death of all deaths!' Oh, foolish men, whose minds turn only to the body, who cannot turn their souls to anything but that which is of the body! Oh, unwise men, who would try to dash the lion's prey from his claws!

Ivo Karajich had only intended to wash and shave at the Fuchses'. But it was not yet six, and when he lay down to rest a while on the couch, he fell asleep in the warm room and slept almost two hours.

A man who has slept has a better grasp of events and their relative importance, and in the morning things take on, if not a different shape, at least a different colour.

He had made a mistake, creating a panic against Hanele's express wishes, and that had made things worse for both of them. He had insulted her father (what disgraceful rudeness, and what lack of discretion, too!). That could not be undone. Should he obey Hanele's advice now, leave the place under even worse conditions, and rely upon their not being able to talk her round in this environment, and further, on their not using force to prevent her from escaping? No, he would not do that. The prize was too dear to him . . . Then there was nothing left but force . . . Ivo Karajich was still determined to go that far, though prepared to limit force to the absolute minimum and as far as possible to keep the authorities out of it. In the meantime he would make one more attempt at negotiation. He would go to fetch Hanele.

When he came out of the house a young man was standing in the street wearing an elegant topcoat dating from the previous century, with flared skirts; perhaps it had been begged, perhaps bought in some small-town sale. Hands in his pockets, he stared at Ivo Karajich with unusual rudeness. Ivo Karajich looked him up and down and their eyes met. There was a green gleam in the youngster's eyes.

Ivo Karajich set out down the road. He had the uncomfortable feeling the young man was following him. On his way he met Andrij Dvujlo.

'Are the men to stay on guard?' asked Dvujlo.

'Yes. If any man is tired he can send somebody in his place. Double their pay! Is the girl still in that place in the orchard?'

'Nobody has seen her, but she seems to be there.'

As Ivo Karajich turned to go on his way, he saw that the young man in the fancy topcoat was standing close behind him. He was standing aggressively, with his legs apart, scowling at Ivo.

Ivo Karajich felt his blood beginning to boil. 'If I don't box that kid's ears today I'll never raise my hand again in my life,' he thought to himself.

Remembering what he had resolved, however, he turned and went the other way.

The kid was Shloym Katz. In a few steps he overtook Ivo Karajich, gave him another threatening scowl as he passed him, and then turned around no more.

Was it the day of the fair? No, Polana was not a market town, Ivo Karajich reminded himself. Pilgrimages and St Martin's Fair were not at this time of year, either! A funeral? A wedding?

There were a lot of people in front of the Shafars' house. They stood about, moving from one group to another or walking up and down, and made little noise as they talked. Most of them were Jews, but there were some Ruthenians too. In their sheepskin coats, men and women alike, they stood together behind the Moskals' cottage fence and waited in silence as though a wandering acrobat was about to begin his performance, or a grand procession arrive.

Is all this in my honour? Ivo Karajich felt his heart beat faster.

His arrival was met by a sudden silence. Most of the bodies turned to face him and all eyes were fixed on him. He sensed curiosity rather than hostility in them. At a pace which tried to show more energy than he really felt he passed through the crowd to get to the millstone steps. The lad in the fancy topcoat stood in his way, and Ivo Karajich was forced to walk a semi-circle around him. If I don't box that kid's ears . . .

Ivo Karajich went into the tap-room which was full of Jews. 'Where is Mr Shafar?' he asked almost too sharply.

One of those waiting there happened to be Baynish Zisovich, who came up to him with a bow and a polite wave of the hand, motioning him towards the kitchen door, which he opened for the newcomer. 'This way, please.'

Leading him across the empty kitchen he opened the door to the parlour. 'In here, if you please.'

What sort of a place had Ivo Karajich landed himself in? From this more than half-empty room, cold and white with its bare walls in the morning sun, eleven pairs of eyes fell upon him and held him fast, like robbers on a bridle path.

The *beder* Moyshe Kahan stood in the room, hat on head, with Leyb Abrahamovich, his lion's mane standing on end, Srul Nakhamkes, the black-complexioned smith, Gutman Davidovich, Mordecai Yid Feinermann, accompanied by his sons, old Yossl Eizigovich, and so on, all ten. One of the twelve of the elders of the Jewish community, Pinches Yakubovich, was missing. The eleventh was – Mr Solomon Fuchs. How many dozen years was it since he had last entered this house? Duty and official business had brought him here now. Had he ever thought he would have the satisfaction of gazing at the poverty and emptiness of this house that he remembered so full of riches?

Ivo Karajich stood face to face with eleven unknown countenances. Who were these eleven men? . . . A secret court of judgement?

'Where is Mr Shafar?' he asked grimly,

'He will be here immediately, Mr Karajich,' Solomon Fuchs answered him.

'Ah! My landlord!' Ivo Karajich said to himself, not without a gleam of satisfaction, being glad to see a face he knew. Deciding nevertheless to go away, and turning towards the door, he saw the way was blocked by two men – Baynish Zisovich and young Eizigovich.

At that moment an old man with a long beard yellowed with age, and white sidecurls down to his shoulders, stepped forward. 'My dear sir,' said Mordecai Yid Feinermann, 'lend your ears for a moment to an old Jew whose days are numbered.' Unable to speak Czech, the old man tried to adapt his Yiddish to German, and it was easy to follow.

In such an unexpected situation, out of the blue, you lose your presence of mind. 'Willingly, if it will not take too long,' Ivo Karajich replied. 'What can I do for you?'

'We are the elders of the Jewish community of Polana, sir, and we wish to offer you our sincere welcome. Sincere and respectful welcome, sir.'

'That is very kind of you. I am glad to meet you,' he shook hands with the old man. 'I shall be delighted to make your acquaintance, but at the moment I am looking for Mr Shafar. You seem to be aware why I am here. I have come to fetch my bride, Hanele.'

With the exception of the old man the judges smiled politely. Solomon Fuchs's smile was broad and intimate.

'I am looking for her,' Ivo Karajich went on. 'You, gentlemen, are perhaps aware, too, that Miss Shafar is of age and that neither you nor anybody else has the right to keep her here by force.'

'Oh! . . . Oh! . . .' the old man held his hand up in front of the speaker, as if to fend something off indignantly. 'Keep her here by force . . .! Who could think anything of the sort? You are wrong, sir. Yossl Shafar will be here. Hanele will be here, too, that lovely girl with the eyes of a gazelle, the most delightful young woman for miles around. And we have met here together in order to rejoice with you and to give you the blessing of the whole of our community. We wish to ask something of you. You see, the girl has no dowry. Allow her to become the daughter of the whole of Israel, for each of us to contribute according to his means to fit her for the wedding, and for us to take the ceremony upon ourselves. My sweet sir,' and the old man, coming closer to Ivo Karajich, gently laid the tips of his fingers on the younger man's coat, 'my dear sir, oh! what a wedding it will be, such as this land has never seen, a *baldachin** more magnificent than any before.'

What amazing perseverance, what obstinacy! Ivo Karajich was struggling with his emotion as he looked into the sad, clever and determined eyes of the old man. 'It would perhaps be beautiful that way,' he said gently, 'but the condition you wish me to accept is beyond my powers.'

Mordecai Yid Feinermann was going on as though he had not heard. 'You are a Jew, sir, just as we are Jews. You are from a great line, of the name of Cohen, the line from which sprang those who once a year were allowed to utter the ineffable name of the Lord. Yet you say: there is no God. There is, sir!' Ivo Karajich saw the old man's eyes begin to blaze. 'There is a God. The one and the only, the unfathomable, whose beginnings may not be questioned.'

'Oh yes, may not be questioned, that's the root of all religions!' His free-thinking blood was roused, and Ivo Karajich would have liked to have said it out loud, but then he waved it aside; what point was there in starting an argument here? Mordecai Yid Feinermann seemed well-informed of his talk with Joseph Shafar the evening before.

'In your youth, sir, you may have heard of the sufferings of Israel for their God since the destruction of the

Temple, for He alone gives them strength to prevail, strength that cannot be but human. You may not have heard of our sufferings here, sir. Come into our homes and see the poverty there, see the hunger of our little ones and watch them die, look at our mothers who have no milk for their babes, and if your heart be not of stone, you will weep.' The old man's eyes filled with tears. 'Ach . . . ach . . . ach . . . sir, and yet you say: there is no God! How could we bear to go on living, did we not know that we are suffering for His sake? Ach, ach, sir; you desire that one of us, even if it be but a girl, should rise and by her deeds cry out: "Perish, oh Israel! All that you have lived for since the creation has been illusion! Your sufferings are but to provide fools and children with laughter! Perish, men of Polana, in your poverty and despair! Behold, I, Hannah, am forsaking you, go on and die, die, I am happy and laughing, I am going out into the world, the world of pleasure and delight; I can do this thing, for there is no requital either in this world or the next, because there is no God!" Ach . . . ach . . . ach . . . sir! . . .' With horror in his eyes the old man held his palms out towards the stranger and retreated slowly backwards.

Terrible, terrible! thought Ivo Karajich to himself, like that day in the streets of Ostrava. What a tragedy! Two thousand years have passed without leaving their mark on these people. He was deeply moved. What could he say in reply to this old man with blazing eyes and red spots of holy ecstasy burning in his parchment cheeks? Could words be of any avail here, would not every word fall unheard? Hanele had known it would be like this. And yet she had come here. How great her love for him must be . . . Hanele! Poor Hanele!

'You may say that we are fools to keep His law. We do no one any harm by this, we do not bother about other people, we hold our peace as we have when the nations said this of us for the past two thousand years. Yesterday a son of the house of Cohen said: There is no God! We answer him: God is a Living God! He liveth and the time of His being hath no end. He is the only God and there is no end to His uniqueness. He lived before all things and His beginning knew no beginning. Our God, our Redeemer, the rock of sorrow in the days of our sufferings. Our banner and our refuge, our cup. Glory be to the Lord, the King of the world! . . . And you, son of the line of Cohen, say no more: There is no God! It is more than enough that you say: I do not believe in God. I have not yet known God. I have not yet found God. We do not believe, for we know: He is and He reigns. We do not believe, for we know: He will send the Messiah. He will send Him soon, for the measure of suffering of His people is running over. Today we have come here to say to you and to beseech you: Isaac, son of Joseph, return to thy people! God Himself will reveal Himself to you. We will help you with advice and with prayer. Behold, we are offering you all we have. And it is more than you can realise today.'

The old man had finished. His hands were trembling a little and the red patches on his cheeks above the yellowing whiskers burned dark.

The strength of this delusion, thought Ivo Karajich, the might of it, the danger! Every attempt to reach understanding here between two minds and two speeches more different than the language of fish and the language of birds, is vain and useless before it begins. He stood there without answering, and with but one thought: I must get away from here! Back to Europe. Poor Hanele!

Solomon Fuchs left the little group and came close to Ivo Karajich. Tossing his head scornfully and shaking his hand loose, he said softly in a confidential business tone of voice: 'Don't mind, Mordecai, Mr Karajich, he's old-fashioned and he doesn't know what the world is like nowadays. Come into the next room with me for a few moments and there is no doubt we can come to terms. You don't know what these village bumpkins of ours are like, it would really be a disaster for us all, it's only a formality, after all . . .'

Ivo Karajich shook his head. He turned to face the old man again. 'Gentlemen,' he said, and felt in advance how tactless if not rude everything he was going to say would be bound to sound. 'I thank you for your kindness and good will; and I thank you especially, sir. I would be very pleased to talk to you about all the matters you have touched on, I fear, though, that it would take rather a long time – these are not matters to be settled in a few words – and it appears that we are not going to agree straight off. I have no time now. I am looking for Hanele Shafar. From your friendly welcome I assume that you are not going to stand in my way. Later I am willing to give you as much time as you wish.'

He opened the door into the next room, the room he had looked into the previous evening; it was empty, as he thought it would be. He guessed where they had hidden Hanele; the Ruthenians had suggested it to him in the night and this morning Dvujlo had confirmed it. In the orchard there was a dilapidated little building put up by Grandfather Abraham, an old cook-house which was used in summer to cook meals for the day-labourers. Hanele was probably there.

Ivo Karajich went out of the room on to the balcony, intending to go down into the farmyard.

He stopped in his tracks. The big farmyard, surrounded by a stone wall, was full of people. Almost every Jew in Polana was there, men, women and children.

At first Ivo Karajich thought their eyes were fixed on him, but he soon realised that they were looking at something behind his back. He turned quickly. The *beder* Moyshe Kahan was standing behind him. He was making some kind of sign to the people, but Ivo Karajich caught sight of the gesture too late.

The crowd was quiet, tense with expectation rather than out to make trouble.

Ivo Karajich stood by the hand-rail along the balcony. He thought for a moment. It was clear that he could do nothing by himself, against four hundred people. Beyond the stone wall of the farmyard he could see the Ruthenians standing behind Moskal's cottage fence and waiting with curiosity to see what would happen. It was none of their business and was nothing more or less than a spectacle for them. On the street he caught sight of two of his men walking up and down, not taking any part in the affair either; it was a matter between the gentleman from the town and the Jews, and they had only been paid to do some watching. They were right and Ivo Karajich was not going to drag them into it.

Then, suddenly, the silence was rent by a murderous cry from the farmyard: 'Kill the dog!'

There was somebody trying furiously to fight his way nearer to the balcony. Ah, it was the youngster in the flared topcoat!

As if infected by the shout a woman's voice scream-ed: 'Send him back where he came from!' That was Brana Yakubovich straining her vocal chords. Then Malke Abrahamovich added her bit: 'Under the sod with him!'

A chorus of boys whistled through their fingers, deafening everyone. Their leaders were Riva Kahan and his faithful follower Benjie.

Shloym Katz was struggling to get through the crowd to the front. Ivo Karajich felt in his pocket for his revolver.

Moyshe Kahan came to the balcony railing and started shouting: 'Shloym, you get back there, quick march! Don't you go letting him through, down there!' He called over to his son Riva: 'You just wait till I get you home!' Shloym Katz shook his fist towards the balcony and hissed something about killing, but the people had formed a barricade to keep him back and grumbling and pushing him they refused to let him get through. Shloym Katz had apparently got ahead of the mood of the crowd; passions had not yet been roused and it was too soon for violence. Brana Yakubovich was the only one whose temperamental outbursts kept pace with his: 'Leave him alone! He's right. Why doesn't the fellow get out of here!' Quiet Moyshe Kahan had been transformed into a lion: 'Horsehead! Horsehead! You know what we have decided on! You, Brana, play the commander in your own home if you like, you're not going to do it here!' The others laughed. 'Why didn't you give your Pinches orders to come along here? Don't you know what you've got to do? Who's responsible here, you or us?'

From the passionate way Moyshe Kahan declaimed his words Ivo Karajich was forced to recognise that he was working the crowd up against him. The *beder* spoke Yiddish and so fast that he could not understand a word of it. The knowledge that he, a commercial traveller, who could hardly be sold out anywhere in Europe, was being sold out here, in his own country, disturbed and angered him.

He leaned his weight on the railing again. 'I have something to say to you, too . . .' he began.

The yard roared with one howling shout. Nobody wanted to hear him speak. The boys put their two fingers in their mouths and started whistling again. Riva turned and cowered to avoid his father's gaze, but Benjie Fuchs was defending the cause of the Lord openly.

Ivo Karajich was used to public speaking and accustomed to stormy meetings. He just stood there calmly and let the crowd give vent to their feelings. He could wait. He looked along the balcony. It was empty. The congregation of the elders had either gone into hiding or gone away.

When the shouts began to die down he spoke again: 'Friends, I shall only say a few words . . .'

The first couple of words ended in a storm of protest. 'We don't want to listen to you!' 'Get out of here!' 'Under the sod with you!' The shouts were in Czech and in Yiddish. Curses rained on him. Ivo Karajich had forgotten this was not one of his meetings. What was at stake was not a political theory. It was God. He was a blasphemer who had come to steal their souls. Once the thought of robbery had entered their minds it spread through the whole crowded yard. 'Child stealer!' 'Child murderer!' The women were screaming the words until they were hoarse.

'Stone him!' The yell was uttered with all the strength and all the force of a man's breath. It was Shloym Katz who was screaming. His eyes were bloodshot and his mouth twisted. A stick flew through the air.

The young people, who had ceased to regard it as entertainment now, took Shloym's cry as their slogan. In the winter, though, there are no stones about, and sticks taken from the pile of firewood, and flung from the middle of the crowd without room for a proper arm swing, either do not reach their target or fall without force.

One of the lads, perhaps a leader of the future, shook himself free of the blinkered thinking of the angry crowd and ran out through the farmyard gate on to the street, shouting: 'Follow me!' A huddle of boys ran after him.

This was just what Ivo Karajich had feared. He had got the closed gate leading from the yard up to the balcony under his observation, but he could be taken by surprise from the other side, from the street.

174

The boys pounded along the balcony. As they came into sight at the corner of the house, Ivo Karajich whipped out his revolver, and aimed it at them.

The boys stopped dead, leaning back on their heels and pressing against those piling up behind them. They stood still. The crowd in the yard, sensing trouble, fell silent.

Ivo Karajich shouted in a loud voice: 'I shall shoot any one of you who takes a step forward.' It sounded calm and convincing.

Another voice broke the silence then, sharp with despair: 'Ivo –' and broke off in the middle, muffled. It was Hanele's voice, coming from the little cook-house in the orchard.

'I'm here, Hanichka, I'm coming!' Ivo Karajich called, holding his weapon before him.

The crowd kept silent. Would the shot come? The boys retreated around the corner.

The first to come to their senses were the mothers of the boys. They set up a terrible screaming, in Yiddish. Not at Karajich, but at their sons. The whole bag of screaming Jewish curses was torn about their ears, mouths were wide open and fists were shaking. The mothers in the crowd were pushing hither and thither wildly, like hens trying to get out. At the corner Moyshe Kahan was cursing the boys, driving them away, and as his son Riva darted off he ran after him.

Taking advantage of the general astonishment, Ivo Karajich went to the railing, putting his revolver away in his pocket and said: 'Friends! I am neither a robber nor a murderer, and I am not going to harm your chil-

dren. I am a peaceable citizen like yourselves. A free,
adult citizen is being held prisoner here. I have come to
fetch her, that is all I want.'

'We won't give her to you!' an elderly man in the
crowd said firmly.

'I am not asking you to do so. I do not want to take
her away. She is not mine and I cannot take her; nor is
she yours, and you cannot give her. Let her decide for
herself! I think that is the just way out.'

They let him say those few words. There were so
many things assaulting their nerves: the revolver, the
boys, the dialogue with the invisible Hanele, his calm
little speech; it was too much, and they needed time to
absorb it all.

Shloym Katz, pale as death, was the first to shout:
'Kill him!' The elderly man called out again, even more
emphatically: 'We won't give her to you!' Then one of
the women, rather belatedly, realised what had just
happened, and shaking off the terror which had run
through her the first moment, squealed shrilly: 'He was
going to shoot us!' Her words were taken up by the
women and the young people like a slogan. 'He was
going to shoot our children . . . kill . . . shoot . . . children . . .'

The Shafars' farmyard suddenly produced a single
sound 'eee' that screamed and squealed and rose and
fell in fury, getting louder and louder and more murderous. The boys who had been driven out on to the street
were whistling shrilly on two fingers, ten, twenty, thirty
of them and the men picked up a militant slogan too and
called out: 'We'll not give her up!' There was 'eee' in

that too, and it was very effective, battering ear-drums and reverberating halfway through the village.

Ivo Karajich remained calm. He listened to the wild fury which, it seemed, would not die down until all four hundred had shouted all the air out of their lungs. He looked at the swelling veins in their necks and the mouths gaping wide, with teeth and without, as if he was watching and listening to something that had nothing to do with him.

Such a strange occurrence! Was he a hero? Or could he guess that what had begun to take a turn for tragedy would yet end well? It must have been that. Ivo Karajich's brain could not get to grips with it, but his very being understood it only too surely and well.

Then the police came on the scene uninvited. The sound of heavy boots clattered along the balcony. A sergeant and three men. Fully armed.

Of course! The previous evening Ivo Karajich had decided to settle the whole business 'as far as possible' without calling in the authorities; that 'as far as possible' was significant. Had he not asked the Ruthenians last night where the police station was, just to be on the safe side?

Or could he imagine that just five minutes' walk away the police could be ignorant of what was going on in the village and what was happening at the Shafars' place? All that day and even in the stormy moments just passed he had not spared them a thought; and yet now he accepted their arrival as something inevitable and planned for, and the fact that they were approaching along the balcony seemed like something he had already envisaged, or at least something he had dreamed of that morning as he lay on the couch at the Fuchses'. True, it was a little strange that the situation should be resolved from quite a different quarter and the fact that the authorities were intervening in his moment of personal heroism and in the argument with God even seemed a little comical – but Ivo Karajich accepted this solution of the crisis with a certain amount of relief.

The three policemen took their stand by the railing facing the farmyard below and their rifle butts rattled to the floor. The sergeant went up to Ivo Karajich.

The hellish row stopped at once. Here and there a shout of 'He was going to shoot at us!' no longer held the threat of murder, but was merely telling tales to a higher authority.

'Silence!' one of the policemen shouted down at them. The police enjoyed unlimited authority there; the silence that fell on the farmyard was complete.

'Who are you, sir?' the sergeant asked briskly, as though he had not just been told by Solomon Fuchs and by Sura.

Ivo Karajich took out his identity papers. As the sergeant slipped them into his pocket another anxious cry came from the old cook-house building, a cry not anxious for itself, but frightened by a silence it could not understand the reason for; this time the cry was complete and unmuffled.

'Ivo!'

'I'm coming, Hanichka!'

'What's going on there?' the sergeant shouted at him. Turning to the men he gave the order; 'Clear the farmyard.' He went to the railing: 'In the name of the law, disperse!' Then, after this ceremonial opening, he roared like a wrathful God: 'This very minute! At the double, be off with you, or as sure as the good God in Heaven is my witness, I'll shoot you to pieces. I'll teach you to start revolutions under my nose!' The sergeant was an old hand, a good strategist, and he knew how to deal with Polana.

The three men with their rifles at the ready ran down the steps into the farmyard to be at the back of the crowd as they jostled towards the gate, and to help them on their way with their bayonets, if required. There would be no need.

Up on the balcony the sergeant thundered after them: 'Want me to come and help you along, Herschko? You get a move on there, Judahorovich!' He wagged a warning finger at Shloym: 'I'll have something to say to you later, my lad!'

A mob that can be called 'Judahorovich' and 'Herschko' and 'Shloym, my lad!' and that realises very well that the sergeant can be a brute over a smoking chimney or a drop of night-soil spilling over into the road or a torch you have forgotten to light on your sledge or the lack of a name-plate on a cart – that is not really a mob at all. A mob that has tasted the joys of power, even if unused, does not like dispersing; they shout, or at least grumble. This Polana crowd did not even grumble. They just jostled faster towards the gate. Riva and Benjie, alone of them all, from the safe distance of a couple of hundred feet from the Shafars', whistled a duet on their fingers, a bold robbers' tune.

179

Ivo Karajich opened the wicker gate on the balcony to go down to the farmyard behind the policemen; the people had all cleared off.

'Hey, you! Where are you off to?' the sergeant shouted after him. 'You can't disappear yet. We've got to report this.'

'I know, sergeant. I'm not going anywhere. I shall be at your disposal whenever you need me.'

The sergeant watched the place being cleared.

Ivo Karajich crossed the yard and went through a little gate into the orchard. He banged loudly on the door of the old cook-house.

'Open this door!' He seized the broken latch and tried to rattle it with unnecessary force, but it came away in his hand and the rusty catch on the inside of the door must have broken off, too; the door opened.

Hanele. Her parents. A woman he did not know, but whose evil look met his eyes for a second. They were all incredibly pale, and Ivo Karajich felt he was looking at the ghosts of the dead. Perhaps the impression was heightened because the little building with its barred window in the cold winter light reminded him of a charnel-house.

'Hanele!'

Her lips moved. Perhaps she breathed the name 'Ivo.'

In one corner with her face to the wall and her hands over her eyes Hanele's mother half lay, half sat. Joseph Shafar stood by the window looking down at the ground.

Why? Ivo Karajich wondered in astonishment, seeing this picture of despair. What disaster had happened, and to whom? My God, what is all this about?

Hanele did not move, either. As if she could not bring herself to take the decision.

'Come, my darling.'

She hesitated for two seconds more. Then she knelt on the ground by her mother and kissed the hair above her temple. 'Goodbye, Mother.'

As she approached her father he lifted his hand and pointed to the door, without taking his eyes from the ground, but the gesture was so weak and halting that again Ivo Karajich felt he was seeing a ghost.

'Goodbye, Father.'

The interrogation by the police, held in the ice-cold tap-room of the house, haunted in its emptiness, was embarrassingly long and bureaucratically stupid – with an obstinacy that does not want to see things as they are, nor people as they are, but insists on following up every detail and nothing but details.

No, replied Ivo Karajich, when the sergeant, realising he had to deal with a man who knew his way about, stopped trying to put the fear of the law into him; no, he did not know any of the local people, he did not understand the language, he was not aware that anyone had threatened him, and he did not bring out his revolver because he had reason to fear the young men, it was only a precautionary measure.

No, replied Hanele, nobody had limited her personal freedom or shut her up anywhere; neither Faiga Kahan nor anyone else had held her by the throat or tried to gag her when she wanted to cry out; yes, she had taken refuge in the old cook-house of her own accord when the crowd gathered; she could have gone away whenever she wanted to and move about as she liked.

'What are those red marks on your wrists?'

'I must have gripped my wrists when the people were shouting.'

'Hmm. Did you grip your mouth as well?'

'I suppose so.'

'It's the old, old story,' said the sergeant. 'The Jews here will never let on against each other as long as they live. We'll get to the bottom of this, though.'

Meanwhile the Ruthenian villagers had come to collect the additional wages Ivo Karajich had promised them. Andrij Dvujlo turned up, too, and Ivo Karajich asked him to pay the bill at the Fuchses' and take their things to Burkal's and get the sledge ready. They would be there soon. The cold house with all its doors ajar was empty and deserted. Hanele's parents had disappeared, and again Ivo Karajich was reminded of a house of the dead. Let's get away from here, away from here as fast as we can, he thought to himself, as the sergeant's pen scratched over the paper in the silence.

At the end of the questioning he asked: 'May we go now, sergeant? Are we free to leave?'

The officer thought the matter over, half-closing his eyes and demonstrating his authority, how only *he* could spare the lovers much embarrassment. Then he said in an official voice, to cover up the fact that he wished them well: 'Well, we've got your addresses. You can go now.'

He turned to his men. 'Fousek and Kraus, accompany these two. Go a bit ahead of them.'

'Thank you, sergeant.'

They left the house. It was noon. On the other side of the road, behind the Moskals' cottage fence, a group of Ruthenians in their sheepskin coats were still standing patiently. A Jewish boy patrolling up and down the road dashed off at a run.

'Didn't you tell him to bring the sleigh up here?' asked Hanele in a quiet voice.

'No, I didn't, Hanichka,' he said a bit guiltily.

She lifted her head and gazed at him with her lovely sad eyes wide open. For a few moments she looked him in the face. 'It would have been quicker. But perhaps it is better this way; we shall pay the penalty for treachery to the bitter end. Do not give me your arm to lean on, my dear, I want to walk down this street of blood alone.'

'What is the matter, Hanichka?' he asked anxiously.

She took a last look around the home of her child-hood.

'Come, Ivo, my dear!'

Next to the Shafars' there were three Ruthenian cottages in their gardens, one on the right and two on the left. Then came the Eizigoviches' cottage. As they came out of the house they heard a strange sound coming from this cottage, a strange rhythm Ivo Karajich could not explain. The nearer they came the more clearly the indeterminate noise took on the sound of the *nigun*, the

183

sad, lamenting, wailing melody of Jewish prayers. Now the lament was full and loud.

The whole of the Eizigovich family had gathered in front of the cottage, women and children, and those who lived at the other end of the village, too. The men, swaying and lamenting in rhythmic chant, were praying the funeral prayer, repeated three times by the people of Israel as the corpse is carried out of the house and sprinkled with vinegar and white of egg: no longer a man, but a piece of unclean flesh already harassed by demons: 'Thus saith Rabbi Akiba: blessed be He for whom Israel keeps itself pure. Who shall purify thee? The Lord in Heaven, who hath said: I will sprinkle you with spring water and you shall be pure and free of all defilement. Turn ye to the Lord, for as the water of the spring cleans all impurities, so the Lord purifies Israel.' Swaying to and fro, turned in on themselves and paying no attention to the unclean thing being swept out from their midst at that very moment, they called out and wailed for the second time: 'Thus saith Rabbi Akiba . . .'

Now came one Jewish cottage after another, and in front of every one the families were gathered and the men were wailing in a loud chorus, each mingling with the next: 'You shall be pure and free of all defilement . . . so the Lord purifies Israel.'

And the outcast walked down the empty street with her impure lover by her side and two Czech policemen ten paces in front of her. She was as white as the path she trod, calling desperately to her aid the blood of her forebears, accustomed to shame and humiliation and suffering, she moved on through the terrible funeral prayers of her grandfather, her face set forward and her eyes fixed in a strange gleam on some far-off point.

They passed the hospitable house of Leyb Abrahamovich, where her friend in the midst of his family sang the funeral prayer in his powerful voice. They walked past the shop of Solomon Fuchs, praying in the midst of his daughters, out to show them the accursed woman, for a memory and a warning to them; and past the Davidoviches' and the Leyboviches' and the Wolfs', and past Mordecai Yid Feinermann with his ceremonial movements in the throng of his sons, his grown-up grandsons and their crowd of women; and past the Katzes' cottage, where the hunchbacked beggar with the handsome head of the Messiah came out to bury her, and where Shloym, with each word of the prayer, tried to drown his own despairing, heartbroken, boyish tears. She walked past one cottage after the other, and the wailing chant of the choirs joined in one terrible grim curse. 'I will sprinkle you with spring water and you shall be pure and free from all defilement.'

Oh, blood of her forebears, spat upon, harried, torn by a thousand blows, do not let Hanele fall!

Step by step, unaware that she moves with proud gait, she passes down the cruel street between Grandfather's funeral prayers, and sees nothing but the whiteness before her.

After the quiet of a couple of Ruthenian cottages, where the chorus could only be heard faintly, Hanele and her lover reached the cottage of Pinches Yakubovich. The *lamet vav*, too, had come out with Brana and the children, to pray beneath the ash trees. Pinches

Yakubovich, as he gazed at the young girl going towards a death worse than the armed man, worse than fire and the grave, towards the death of all deaths, spiritual death, did not see what the rest of Polana saw.

Behold the scapegoat of the Lord, that hath taken away the sins of Israel! She alone in the name of all! Behold the greatest sacrifice of all, laid upon the altar of the Lord as a solemn peace-offering. Great, eternal, holy and unfathomable is God the Lord of Hosts. Praise be to His name!

Thus Hanele, the first in the history of all Polana, forsook her father's house and the place of her Lord.

Then she felt someone lift her up and sit her down on something soft and springy and scented.

Grandfather's funeral melody had died away and the silence that succeeded it was infinitely lovely and kind.

She heard Ivo say: 'Thank you, gentlemen.'

Then she felt a slight jerk, felt the air blowing past her cheeks, heard the tinkle of the bells and the thunder of the hooves. They were driving away. She kept her eyes closed. Oh, they were driving away.

Far, far away! she said to herself, like young children at play.

She felt for his hand to see if Ivo was beside her, and her hand touched his for a second. His hand, which had left her in peace, mistakenly thinking it was being asked for sympathy, came closer to her. Hanele pushed it away again.

She opened her eyes. The horses were thundering down the narrow valley, where there was only a road and a stream frozen far out from its banks, and only down the middle where the transparent water still flowed was it strangely green; otherwise there were only wooded mountainsides covered in snow, and a narrow strip of sky above their heads.

Hanele barely glanced at the scene around her. She fixed her eyes on that strip of sky: on the grey tumult of clouds pouring along like the stream beneath, rolling on in waves and rushing down from the hills to the valley, like the river. Hanele's wide-open eyes rested there, and the man at her side, understanding her, did nothing to draw them away.

'Grandfather!' she whispered. For that name was the only thing that came up from the dark depths within her.

At home her father, dishonoured for ever, slashed the lapel of his coat with a knife and tore it, and her mother, who would never again leave the house or orchard, ashamed to show herself before her fellows, now tore the garment at her throat. Barefoot, they sat on the ground, weeping over the death of their youngest daughter, to chant the prayer for the dead; while Hanele fixed her eyes on a strip of snow clouds, and those beautiful eyes drank in the sorrow of the sky.

And as the red sun sank behind the mountains of Polana and ten men gathered in the dark synagogue to pray for the dead, Hanele was driving out through the gate of the mountains into the gleaming plain lit by that same sun that was still shining in all its glory here; and her eyes poured on with the clouds into a great lake, where the waves tossed stormily only where the mountain stream flowed into it, and further and further away it grew calmer and calmer, until on the horizon it was still and clear. Hanele's eyes drank in this breadth and endless space, too.

The next day, when the town rabbi was lighting a black candle for her in the synagogue, Hanele was speeding along a frozen road lined with a sprinkling of powdery snow, in a yellow car with a big box at the back; and the road led past vineyards where tiny houses like cardboard toys stood among the naked poles, and she was dashing through villages where there were big crosses on the village churches and children playing in front of little Jewish shops. This was later, when Hanele could begin to think again, and remember. This was the time when something hard and obstinate entered her eyes.

This sorrow, this far-away dreaminess, and this grain of hardness caught in it, will be in her eyes for ever. In those wonderful eyes which may one day be handed down to the children of Hannah Karajich.

Notes

These Notes were compiled by Marcela Hajek, in consultation with the General Editor.

Page 3 – *Polana:* a remote village in the mountainous part of Ruthenia where Hannah Karajich grew up among the closely knit orthodox Jewish community. It is a name that frequently occurs in the Carpathian region and denotes a village situated high up in the mountains.

Page 3 – *goy:* Gentile, not Jewish.

Page 3 – *How different it looks spelt that way* (i.e. Hanichka, née Shaffer): Hannah Shafar was the original Yiddish spelling of the maiden name of Ivo Karajich's young wife.

Page 4 – *Mukachevo:* as a major industrial and commercial centre of Ruthenia, this lively town attracted people with money and aspirations.

Page 4 – *Hanele:* this is the affectionate Yiddish diminutive of Hannah, as opposed to the Czech diminutive 'Hanichka'.

Notes

Page 4 – *Count Palugyay and Pálfy and Berceny:* well-known aristocrats and public figures in the Austro-Hungarian empire.

Page 4 – *Ruthenian:* this refers to the local, non-Jewish inhabitants of Ruthenia. See the Introduction to this volume.

Page 5 – *His Lordship:* the Czech original – *knize* – literally means 'the Count', who owned the land around Polana.

Page 5 – *guilder:* the Austrian and German currency (gold and silver coins) of the period. There were two guilders to the crown, the Austrian monetary unit of the late nineteenth and early twentieth century. The crown became the basic Czechoslovak monetary unit and is still in use in the Czech Republic today.

Page 5 – *heller:* a coin of low denomination. There were 100 hellers to the crown.

Page 6 – *Edmond Egan* (1851–1901): a high official of Irish origin who, at the end of the nineteenth century, was given powers by the Hungarian government to introduce major industrial and agricultural reforms in the province.

Page 8 – *shiva:* seven days of mourning for a close relative following a funeral.

Page 9 – *the language of the Lord:* i.e. Hebrew.

Notes

Page 11 – *gemilut khasadim:* charity.

Page 11 – *Herschko:* the Ukrainian diminutive variant of Hersch.

Page 12 – *tallith:* a shawl, usually white with black stripes, worn by Jewish men in the synagogue.

Page 13 – *the war:* i.e. The First World War.

Page 15 – *Whom did Polana belong to?:* In 1918–19 it was unclear whether the victorious Allies would leave Sub-Carpathian Ruthenia in Hungary or assign it to the new state of Czechoslovakia.

Page 18 – *beder:* ritual bathhouse attendant, a significant office in the local Jewish community.

Page 31 – *mikvah:* ritual Jewish bath.

Page 39 – *'Gute woch'* and *'Gut shabos':* the first greeting (Good week) is used after the Sabbath, the latter (Good Sabbath) on Friday before the holy day.

Page 39 – *Yom Kippur* and *Rosh-ha-shanah:* the Day of Atonement – Yom Kippur – is an annual Jewish holy day marked by fasting and prayer. It is observed on the tenth day after the festivities of Rosh-ha-shanah, the New Year of the Jewish calendar.

Page 50 – *ma'ariv:* evening prayer for protection during the night, read when the stars appear.

Page 52 – *halutz:* young Zionist pioneers who trained for settlement in Palestine.

Page 53 – *galuth:* diaspora, dispersed Jews who live outside Palestine.

Page 59 – *shohet:* a person who performs the ritual of slaughtering animals according to the Jewish law.

Page 60 – *elections:* the newly established Czech administration very much depended on the Jewish vote. The Jews – less than a tenth of the population – represented a better organised and a more influential group, both financially and economically, than the mainly poor Ruthenian peasants and shepherds. The rabbis, with their tight control over their religious communities, held the key. Favours were expected on both sides.

Page 61 – *District Commander:* the chief district administrator.

Page 61 – *mizrakhi:* a strictly religious Zionist group of local youth which was formed to outmanoeuvre the more politically oriented mainstream Zionist movement.

Page 64 – *barkhes:* plain wheat-flour pastry, usually plaited or twisted, which is eaten during the Jewish holidays.

Page 64 – *Riboinoi shel oilom!:* Yiddish form of Hebrew exclamation: Ribonoh shel olam! Lord of Creation!

Notes

Page 67 – *lamet vav* (literally 'thirty-six'): a reference to the thirty-six sages without whom – according to Jewish legend – the world could not exist. They reappear every generation and live unrecognised among people as well as being unknown to each other.

Page 72 – *nigun:* tune, song or rhythm.

Page 72 – *hakhshara:* preparation for life and work in Palestine or the location where it takes place.

Page 85 – *havduleh:* a ceremony performed at the end of the Sabbath or the holy days which separates them from the other weekdays.

Page 93 – *kedma:* premises allocated for *hakhshara,* that is, where preparation for living and working in Palestine takes place.

Page 94 – *treyfe:* ritually unclean, not kosher, unfit for consumption by orthodox Jews.

Page 95 – *Hanichka or Anna:* these are her Czech names. Within the Jewish community of her native Polana the Shafars' daughter was called Hanele or Hannah.

Page 99 – *betarka:* a female member of Betar, a radical Jewish organisation.

Page 115 – *mezzuzah:* a little case containing a parchment scroll inscribed with extracts from the Old Testament, attached to the right-hand doorpost of Jewish homes.

Notes

Page 123 – *tefillin:* phylacteries, a pair of small, black leather boxes in which parchment scrolls with the Old Testament verses are kept. They are provided with leather straps and by means of leather thongs are bound to the head and left arm of Jewish men during weekday morning prayers.

Page 131 – *Prevoskhodityelstvo:* Excellency (in Russian).

Page 167 – *baldachin:* a wedding canopy. The Hebrew term is 'hupah'.